Before The Love

Sexy Stories Collection

VOLUME 19

10 EROTIC SHORT STORIES

EMILIE HAMDAN

Publisher's Note: This is a work of fiction. Names, characters, places, and incidents are a product of the author's imagination. Locales and public names are sometimes used for atmospheric purposes. Any resemblance to actual people, living or dead, or to businesses, companies, events, institutions, or locales is completely coincidental.

Before The Love/ Emilie Hamdan. -- 1st ed.
Xplicit Press, an imprint of TLM Media LLC

ISBN-13: 978-1-62327-550-1
ISBN-10: 1-62327-550-4
eISBN: 978-1-62327-600-3

Printed in the United States of America

CONTENTS

1 TEMPEST'S FIRE

By the age of fifteen, Tempest had been bounced around from foster home to foster home, for eight years. Her father had abandoned her and her mother when she was seven. Then, her mother lost custody of her and her brothers, after leaving them home alone for four days. She'd been so high that she forgot she had children.

Tempest Smothers was born in Detroit, Michigan. She had been left to take care of her two brothers, ages five and two. The neighbors began to suspect something was wrong when they discovered her youngest brother outside, in nothing but a diaper. It was mid-winter and this horrified the residents of 457 Wilson Ave.

Jane Salmon was a nosy neighbor,

anyway. Yet, upon finding the child, she scooped him up and went to their apartment, to confront the "unfit bitch"! Only, instead of finding Tempest's mother, she found Tempest and Dylan, alone. All three kids were filthy and unfed. The apartment was filthy. The six cats had relieved themselves everywhere and the kids were living off of peanut butter and moldy bread.

The conditions were appalling. The law was there in a heartbeat. Tempest and her brothers were rescued, but she never saw her brothers, or mother, again. Placed into foster care, Tempest felt alone and abandoned. Her temper often got her into trouble and the families didn't know what to do with her. Then, when she was fifteen, she lived with a foster dad who thought she could make him happy, in inappropriate ways.

The last night at the Birmingham's, Ed had attempted to make Tempest his own. Tempest would have nothing to do with it. The fire within her ignited and she beat the shit out of the old man. Disgusted and afraid, she ran out of the house and never looked back.

The cops were called on her, but she gave them the slip.

Now, in her early twenties, Tempest's life was a mess. She'd kept free of street drugs and she escaped prostitution, early.

When she turned 19, she changed her trade. She began to dance. She was pretty good at it, too.

Her sassy, auburn hair played teasingly, with the fluorescent lights of the strip bar. Men loved her. Her long, sexy legs were firm and sensual. She was willing to let them touch, for a few bucks more, but never went too far.

At Misty's Bar, Tempest made good money. She had a decent place, a rather nice car, and her furry feline friend, Tuffy.

Sitting upon the fire escape, just outside her bedroom window, Tempest took a drag of her smoke and exhaled it, slowly. Her hand trembled, as she thought about her brothers. They'd been close. She hoped they'd found a good life.

She sipped thoughtfully on her Diet Coke and sighed. Tuffy, her ever-faithful friend, joined her on the ledge, and rubbed his body against her as he purred loudly.

"You're the only man in my life that I can count on," she told him.

Tuffy replied with a purr and a tiny sandpapery lick of the tongue, upon her cheek.

"Gee thanks, Tuff... I needed that."

Dylan Williams stood at the front of the church and read from the Bible, quoting his father's passage of choice. The young ladies of the church were dressed like little virgins, clean and pure. The congregation had much esteem for Dylan, who was considered a genuine “good boy.”

Dylan stood 6 feet, 2 inches tall. He had light brown hair and silver blue eyes, with a modest physical build. Not overly muscular, but his ability to ride horses and climb rocks provided him with a certain, natural, sex appeal. He was the youngest of six and the only male in the bunch. His world was full of women. Mom had taught him to treat women with respect and dignity. However, he kept it modestly disguised.

Greta Banks, the nosiest busybody of all, often knew everything about everyone. Fact, or not, if she heard it she blabbed it. The women at Jenny’s Salon called her the town’s enquirer. Anyone wanting to know anything could ask Greta. Yet, for the most part, it was simply nothing more than nasty rumors and gossip.

However, for the few moments of reverent mention, it would have been evil, but they justified their gossip by calling it “prayer worthy information.” After all, the more information God had, the better the prayer would be.

Greta also had a daughter, Melanie. She was an average-looking, wholesome good girl. From the day Greta met the Reverend’s son, she was determined to have Dylan as a son-in-law.

Melanie was a simple girl. Bright

enough, but a plain Jane. Not allowed to wear make-up, show her legs above the knee, arms were never shown below the elbow, head was always covered in church, and above all, she was never to be seen alone, with anybody, after dark. The only boy worthy of her daughter was Dylan.

Dylan, on the other hand, didn't like Melanie, at all. He was kind enough to her. It's how he was raised. Yet, Melanie never took a hint.

Dylan was a do-gooder and happy to help anyone in need. Sometimes, something inside him screamed for freedom, whatever that meant.

Tempest completed her shift at Misty's Bar, and had thickly lined her pockets once again. Yet, like always, she'd come home alone. Knowing that Tuffy would be there to greet her gave her strength to turn the key to her apartment.

Normally, when the sounds of the key clicked, Tuffy would run from the couch he hogged to greet Tempest at the door. When Tempest opened the door, she was immediately surprised to see that Tuffy wasn't there to greet her.

She called for him. "Tuffy? Tuffy boy, where are you?"

She made kissy-kissy sounds to encourage his appearance. Then, she walked to the couch to look for her friend. The moment she saw him, she knew. His body was still and rigid. His eyes partially glazed and whitened. His lips gaping and still. Tuffy was dead.

"NO!" She cried, hysterically. "Oh, Tuffy..." She sobbed, relentlessly. "Why, why, why?" She asked herself, over and over.

Tuffy was an older cat she'd rescued from the street. He wasn't a kitten, by any means, but he'd been a loyal friend. Now, in his senior years, he'd parked on Tempest's couch, until his last breath.

Tempest gained just enough composure to collect her deceased cat and carry him to the park, for a proper burial. Three o'clock in the morning, in one of the most dangerous parks in Detroit, and Tempest was outside, burying her cat.

With her fingernails, now caked with dirt, and her face stained with tears, she painfully said, "Good-bye, Tuffy," one last time.

As she strolled back, towards her home, an overwhelming sense of loss and pain engulfed her very soul. She was alone. The only friend she had, in the whole world, was gone and all she had to hold on to, now, was her job. A job she knew would pay the bills, but never fulfilled her, at all.

As she dragged herself back, over the bridge to her apartment, the pains of her life began to swell within her head. Her life was in shambles and she had no one to love. She'd used all the strength she had to make it to this day, but the thought of another pain-filled day ate at her, dreadfully.

"I can't do this anymore. I just can't!"

Suddenly, the floods of bad memories came flooding back. Mom and her habit, the loss of her brothers, the many foster homes, the molestation from her foster dad, the many nights of turning tricks just to have a meal, the nights of dancing in scanty display, it was all she'd known of her worth.

With her heart and head wreathing with grief and misery, she numbingly began to climb upon the bridges ledge. As tears fell from her face, a kind and warm voice spoke to her.

"Please, don't jump," he said.

Startled, she turned around a little, nearly losing her footing. She wanted to jump, but she was simply working on the nerve to do it.

Looking into her desperate eyes, Dylan spoke, again. "Please. Come down." He extended his hand and smiled, with sincere compassion. She was confused.

"Who are you?" She sniffed.

"Dylan. My name is Dylan. What's

yours?"

She looked back, down at the water, and stood quietly for a moment.

"Listen," he said. "I certainly do not want to see you jump and I can see you are upset. But, if you would like to give me a chance to talk you out of it, I'd like to do that."

"Talk me out of it? How are you going to do that?" She asked.

"Truth?"

She waited.

"Truth is, I don't really know what to say, but I am a good listener."

She stood silently, sizing him up.

"Listen, why not come down here... at least, for the moment, and see if we can't find a solution that doesn't involve jumping into the river. Can we do that, please?" His voice was sincere and warm. "Just give me your hand. I will help you down. Then, just take it one-step at a time. Okay?"

She hesitantly nodded. Then, taking his hand, she knelt down, until he could help her off the ledge and place her firmly back upon the solid ground.

"Ah," he sighed. "Thank you."

"For what?"

"Not making me jump into the river after you," he confessed. "I hate water! Terrified!"

"Really?" She asked. "I love it! I swim

every chance I can. At least, I use to."

He smiled warmly, again. "I know it's late, but can I buy you a coffee, or something? We could talk inside at Tim's. They have the best chocolate cupcakes in the world." He said, enticingly.

"Mmm, chocolate?" She smiled. "You must know how women think."

"Having five sisters might have something to do with that…" He smirked.

She laughed. "I imagine so. I hope you had more than one bathroom in the house!"

"We had two and I still had to fight for a moment to myself," he laughed.

After Tempest washed up in the lady's room, she and Dylan sat down inside the coffee shop and Tempest embraced the sweet morsel, with a tantalizing, "Mmm!" The cupcake's inner warmth of chocolate ganache slithered, slowly down the back of her throat, with an arousing smoothness. "Heavenly!" She said, almost forgetting about her surroundings.

"So, Tempest…" Dylan said.

She opened her eyes, as she returned from her alluring moment of ecstasy. "Yea?"

"Can you tell me…?"

"Tell you what?"

"You were out quite late, bad neighborhood, covered in dirt, ready to jump...."

"Oh... that," she scoffed. She paused, feeling foolish. "I'd rather enjoy the cupcake..."

He smiled. Then, let her compose her thoughts. "I'm listening..."

Tempest sighed, for a moment, as she struggled to choke back the tears. "Just a bad day, I guess..."

"Day?"

"I've had a string of bad luck, hard lumps, but tonight, my best friend died and it just tore me to shreds."

"I'm sorry," Dylan said, empathetically. "How did it happen?"

"I don't know. Guess it happened in his sleep."

"Gracious. That'd be tough...was he very old?"

"Hmm...not really sure. Maybe, fifteen or sixteen," she replied.

"God that's terrible! His parents must be devastated!"

Suddenly, Tempest realized what Dylan was thinking. Then, with an uncontrollable release, she burst into hysterical laughter. Dylan was shocked. "Her friend's dead, his family's grieving, and she's laughing?" He thought.

The look on his face, a look of concern and wonder, only increased her need to laugh. Tears began to flood from her eyes.

"Are you okay?" He asked.

With everything she had in her, she composed herself. "I am so sorry… I didn't mean to laugh like that," she confessed.

"Well, I guess everyone deals with grief differently. I was just surprised…I mean…laughing when a kid dies!" Dylan was still weirded out.

"Not a kid. My cat!" She said. "Tuff, my cat died!"

"What?"

"That's what I was doing in the park… burying my cat," she said. "I know I should have taken him to a vet, or something, but I couldn't. So, I buried him in the park."

"Oh man, now, I got it!" Dylan understood how it would be funny.

Their laughter broke the ice. They soon became quite comfortable with each other's company. They talked for hours, about everything. She talked about her life and he talked about his. Hers was less than perfect and his was too, seemingly, perfect.

Then, as the sun came up, Dylan walked Tempest home.

"Can you come up?" She asked.

"I'll fix us breakfast," she offered.

"I probably shouldn't," he said. He knew his father would never approve, but he wanted to. He really wanted to.

"Dylan Williams!" Shouted a voice. "What are you doing here?"

Suddenly, he turned around and saw Greta Banks. She stood, stout as ever, with her fancy hat and pocketbook, with her nose turned upwards. Her eyes moved up and down Tempest, with animosity and disgust.

"Mrs. Banks, how are you?"

"Hmm..." She snooted. "I am fine, but what are you doing here, with this girl? One of your charity cases?"

"Mrs. Banks, for the love of God, just once in your life... Mind your own business!"

Her mouth dropped. "Dylan! What's gotten into you?" Then, with a cold distain, she scowled at the pretty redheaded girl. "Jezebel! You've planted your devilish wiles upon the Reverend's son! You'll rot!"

"Reverend?" Tempest replied.

"Mrs. Banks, you better leave while I still have my NICE guy on," he said, with emphasis.

"But I..."

"NOW!"

Greta gasped. Totally floored by his distain, she huffed with fury and stormed off, towards her hair appointment.

"I can just hear the gossip now..." Dylan said.

"Gossip?" Tempest asked.

"She is the biggest and busiest, nosiest… ah!"

"I'm sorry if this gets you into trouble."

"Not to worry. She's not anyone I worry about."

"No, I mean with your father. A reverend?"

"He is. Yes."

"I can't be responsible for getting you in trouble with…."

Dylan quickly placed his finger upon her lips. "Tempest… Don't worry about it."

"But I…" She choked. What had she done? Her whorish ways had brought shame to the son of a holy man. "Damn it, girl!"

"Don't worry about it. Really!" He grabbed her shoulders, gently, and looked her square in the eyes. "I'm not anywhere I don't want to be. Okay?"

Tempest opened her eyes, but there were no words to say.

"Now… Didn't you say something about making us some breakfast?" He asked.

Hesitantly, she smiled. "You sure?"

"Absolutely!"

She nervously fumbled with the lock to the building and led him inside, behind her. Mrs. Banks, who'd been watching from afar, gawked with disgust. "Harlot!" She scolded, just as a group of ladies walked down the street, behind her. Her words alarmed them. "That boy needs prayer!"

She quickly stormed into the salon and saw some of her regular friends there. Immediately, she began talking about the harlot that lured the preacher's son to the lioness' lair. The women were horrified.

Alice Corson interjected. "Maybe, there's nothing to it."

"You're naïve," said Greta. "The woman has clearly lured men, like this, to her lair before. Poor good men, led astray, by the skin she flaunts."

The women hung on every word, as Greta shared the story with them.

While Greta was busy talking up a cloud of bull, Tempest was busy flipping the eggs, sizzling the bacon, and browning up the home fries. She stood, sweet as an innocent child who'd just met Santa Claus for the first time. Something about Dylan was making her feel young again. She felt less like trash and more like someone special.

As she continued to cook, they spoke more and more, about the things they liked and didn't like, the woes of the street and the woes of a religious community. Yet, somewhere in the middle, they learned something they liked about the other side. Dylan's life was rigid and

Tempest's life had no stability. Despite their very different worlds, a kindling was beginning to form.

"Wow, these are some of the best eggs and home fries I've ever had!" He boasted.

"Yeah?" She asked, bashfully.

"Oh for sure!" He replied, taking another bite. "You like cooking?"

"I like it a lot!"

"You should consider being a chef, or something."

She sighed. "I don't know..."

"You have no faith in yourself, do you?"

She shrugged.

Dylan stood up, from the table, and approached Tempest, who leaned against the counter, casually. "You're a special person. So, you've had a few bad things happen... Some terrible things, in fact. But, you can't be ruined. You're still too nice a person to be ruined. A little love and healing, and you'll be the very person you were meant to be." He said.

He said it with such conviction, she almost believed him. "You really think so?"

"I know so!"

"I..."

"Shh..." He gently placed his finger on her lips, again. Then, he moved in, to kiss them, gently. "You are one very special lady. Don't forget it!"

Then, he kissed her, again. Then again, but this time, she returned the kiss, with sincerity. She carefully placed her hands around his shoulders and surrendered to his gentle touch.

He was new at this, but he didn't care. Despite her history, Dylan made her feel like a virgin bride, being loved for the very first time.

Dylan carefully placed his hands upon her face and ran his fingers through her silky hair. He moved in to kiss down her neck. She sighed. He continued to kiss down the front of her body, moving down, toward her chest. The silky tank felt nice beneath his fingers, as he gently placed his hands upon her breasts.

She moaned.

"I'm sorry... Should I stop?" He asked.

"No, please don't."

Dismissing the words of his youth, he continued to stroke the cup of her soft, perky breasts. Then, as the nipples perked in excitement, Dylan smiled, curiously. Tempest moved her fingers to the top of his shirt and began to unbutton it. As she began to move her fingers down the shirt, she got to see the smooth, firm pecks beneath. Gently, she moved her fingers along his chest and slid them down to his washboard abs.

She'd had sex before, but Dylan was showing more than just a sexual need. He was sharing a love for her. He then moved his fingers under the silky top and gently lifted it over her head, revealing the rose-colored bra beneath it. Gently, he kissed her down the nape of her neck and moved his hands over her body, stroking her silky smooth skin.

She carefully removed his shirt and gently stroked her fingers down his torso, to his waist. Teasingly, she slipped her fingers into the top and licked his neck. Then, gently, she loosened his buckle and released him of the compressed growth he was feeling beneath.

As she continued to make her way into his pants, he grabbed her ass and held it firmly with one hand. The other hand groped her silky white thigh, as it wandered up and under the tiny black skirt. Her legs were smooth and silky. He was aroused even more, when he discovered her panties and the Brazilian, clean shave underneath.

He raised a brow, with interest, but said nothing. Then, he gently moved his fingers into her clit and discovered the world of the feminine "spot." As he gently stroked her cherry, her moaning began to rise. His interest peaked, more, when the fluids of interest began to emerge beneath his fingers.

Dylan gently slid his fingers through her lips and slipped them into the opening of her vagina. He liked the sounds she made, as he pleased the beautiful girl.

Tempest, then, friskily grabbed his pants and briefs, and pulled them down, hard, releasing the hardened cock within. She stroked it, eagerly, as he finally realized what he'd been missing all this time.

"I don't expect you to have a condom?" She asked.

"Wasn't in my plan," he said.

"Not a problem. She quickly pulled one from the purse she had nearby, and assisted him with applying it. He was so young and immature, he was afraid he'd go off, too early. So, ensuring his ladies pleasure, he continued to stroke her, gently, upon her clit. She moaned, increasingly, as her back leaned back, upon the countertop.

Then, with his interest peaked, he removed the silk panties and relieved the luscious kitten beneath. With his cock ready for penetration, they moved into position with freedom. Her knowledge helped, but despite her experience, her moment with Dylan was very new. He made her feel good, in a way that sex, alone, could not.

With a sweet shift of their bodies, Dylan's penis entered Tempest and moved upward, to her pleasure. He began to stroke it back and forth, as she moaned and gripped against the counter. Her body flexed, with climatic arousal, while his toes curled with ecstasy. As he moved back and forth, his arousal would soon release, but with her still on the rise, he continued to slide it in and out, while he gently moved his fingers along her clit. Her moans climbed and climbed, until her bright eyes rolled back, into her head, and her orgasm erupted into total euphoria.

As the pounding of her heart beat, hastily, with the conclusion of her orgasm, her mind returned to Dylan.

He looked at her, with eyes of insane love. "You're amazing!" He said.

"So are you, Dylan," she replied.

"I'm new. I went too quick… I…"

"The sex was fine, but the loving touch was something I've never known before," she explained.

"Really?"

"You're perfect, Dylan." She lovingly kissed him on the forehead and wiped the sweat from his brow. "Can't imagine what Mrs. Banks is going to do to your life, now, though?" She said, with a moment of regret.

"Oh, screw her! I can deal with her, my dad, everybody! This is MY life and if I want to make hot, steaming love with you the rest of my life, then, that's exactly what I am going to do!"

"Really?"

"Really!"

The patter of her heart changed, from

ecstasy to unfolding love, as they embraced, again, in a kiss. Then, pulling away, for just a moment, Dylan said, "I guess the only way to get good at this is practice. Right?" He winked.

"Right?" She said, with some intrigue.

"Then, maybe, it's time for another lesson." He scooped her up, off the counter, and lovingly carried her down the hall, to her room, where the passion of their fire would continue to mature and grow.

While the fire of Mrs. Banks would be tough to extinguish, the fire in Tempest's eyes was real, and the fire in Dylan's heart was ramped. Neither had regrets. Love had rescued two souls from different worlds and brought a fire nobody would ever tame.

2 BEFORE "I DO"

Tiffany had been dating Chad for nearly a year, and he was head over heels for her. She'd met his parents and he'd met hers. Tiffany's father confirmed that Chad was a good man. He'd be a good provider, a loving and attentive husband, and a terrific father—everything a young woman could want in a husband.

Tiffany didn't deny that he was a great person, and she did love him. Yet she wasn't as much "in love" with him as she'd wanted to be. Still, good men are hard to find, so she joyfully accepted his proposal for marriage.

Chad was a young attorney, fresh out of law school. He'd landed a fantastic job in a large firm, and he liked the opportunities this company would have with his career's growth. Although his salary wasn't what it was going to be, he was already making a decent income. Tiffany would no doubt be cared for.

Tiffany was a beautiful brunette with stunningly dark brown eyes. She'd always taken pride in maintaining good health and was a devout vegan. As a profession, she'd chosen a career in veterinary medicine and later focused on zoology. She'd especially had a passion for elephants and followed her dream to the San Diego zoo. Now she was one of their finest veterinarians. Tiffany was really living the dream. She had the best job, a great family, and a soon to be great husband—with amazing in-laws.

The only member of his family she hadn't met was Chad's sister Kelly. Kelly was a high school teacher in Atlanta. She was older than Chad by just 18 months, and they'd always been pretty close. But since they became busy with college and careers, they'd lost touch somewhat. Emails and texts were sent, but it wasn't the same.

Kelly had heard about Tiffany and was thrilled when she heard her little brother was getting married. Now, with just a few weeks to go before the wedding, it was time to fly home for a visit.

Chad drove to the airport to pick up Kelly, before picking Tiffany up at the zoo. When he finally saw her for the first time in nearly a year, he was ecstatic and so was she. Kelly practically leaped into his arms as they embraced with a joyful hug

"I can't believe it!" Kelly said. She sized him up in his fancy suit. "You look all grown up!"

"So do you, teacher..."

"Well...how do you like being a lawyer, huh?"

"Like it just fine. How do you like working with the kids?"

"Aw, it's great. Sometimes it's a challenge...hmm...actually it's got a lot of challenges, but the rewards outweigh the woes."

"It sure is good to see you, sis!"

"I can't believe my little brother's getting married!"

"I know...crazy isn't it?"

"I can't wait to meet her."

"You seeing anyone?" Chad asked.

"I was, but she and I broke up."

Chad froze in his tracks. "She?!"

"Yeah, I haven't told mom or dad yet."

"When did this happen?"

"During my university years."

"You never said anything before..."

"Wasn't important."

"Well...okay then," Chad immediately accepted Kelly's decision and then proceeded to find her bags. "Shall we go, sis?"

As they entered the back door of the zoo, the place where family—and fiancés—got to enter, they went in search of the wonderful Dr. Tiffany Wilcox. They made their way to the elephant cage and soon found the beautiful brunette in khaki's.

Unaware she was being watched, she began working on the young elephant's ears. She was so caring and attentive that neither Chad nor Kelly wanted to interrupt.

"It's okay, Willy," she said. "It's okay mama, I won't hurt your baby." The elephants seemed to trust her, even though they were edgy about some of the treatments she had to perform. Gently she applied some ointment to a wound behind the baby's ear and then kissed him on the head. "What a good boy you are, Willy. Yes, yes you are!"

Chad and Kelly snickered.

Immediately she turned around in surprise.

"Oh shit Chad, you scared me!"

"Sorry Tiff...you just looked so cute!"

"Thanks...I have elephant slime on my sleeve and I look cute." She looked doubtful, but was happy that he took the time to compliment her. Still speaking through the cage wall, Tiffany said, "Hi...you must be Kelly."

"Yes, I'm Kelly."

"Great! Happy to meet you. I've gotta wash up, then will be right out."

Kelly and Chad sat upon the bench outside the cage and watched the elephants feed and graze. Kelly smiled. "They are fascinating, aren't they?"

"I don't know..." Chad said. "They're not my thing, but Tiffany sure loves them."

"Aw Chad, you gotta admit...they're awfully cute."

"Okay. They're cute."

Tiffany finally emerged from the clinic and was much more presentable. She then carefully gave Chad a hug and kiss.

"You smell like an elephant," he said.

"Gee, thanks!"

"Chad!" Kelly scolded him.

"What?"

"Ah...don't worry about it, Kelly. He's not really an animal lover." Tiffany admitted. "Are you?"

"Oh yes!" Kelly said. "I couldn't do the job you do, but I sure would love a moment or two with these amazing creatures!"

"Really?"

"Sure!"

"Well...maybe sometime before you go back to Atlanta, I will bring you here to meet Tabitha and her baby."

"I'd love that!"

"Okay girls, I think we've had enough elephant talk for the day. We've got a dinner date with mom and pops..."

"Chad, chill man!" Kelly snapped.

"Well, I guess I should get going if I'm going to shower and change before dinner," Tiffany said.

"Sounds like a plan!" Chad said. He knew Tiffany loved the zoo, but Chad could take or leave it. He didn't hate animals, he just didn't care for them with the passion Tiffany had.

After a great shower and some freshening up, Tiffany emerged looking as pretty as could be. She wore her dark hair down, and her makeup was simple and sweet.

"Ready for dinner?" she asked.

"You look great, Tiff!" Chad said.

"Thanks sweetie."

They arrived at the restaurant, where their parents were already gathered. Kelly immediately hugged her parents, and the gentlemen stood while the ladies sat took their seats.

Chad and Kelly's parents—Harvey and Marj—were thrilled to have their family gathered together. Tiffany's folks—Todd and Liz—were equally thrilled.

Harvey stood at the head of the table and began to ting his glass. After gaining everyone's attention, he said, "It's been a joy and privilege getting to know Tiffany this year. She's a true joy and a stunning beauty. Couldn't be happier—well that is until I get an equally wonderful son-in-law!"

Kelly gulped. Chad looked at her quirkily and wondered when she'd tell them the truth about her sexuality.

"This is a joyous celebration; please enjoy this meal on us!" Harvey declared. He began to sit down as the waiter approached to take everyone's order.

"Wait!" Tiffany said, interrupting the dinner party. "I'm sorry..." she said to the waiter. "Can you give me one moment, please?"

He obliged.

"Something wrong, Tiff?" Chad asked.

"No, no." Tiffany reassured him. "I just had to ask Kelly a question, but wanted to ask her with all of you present."

"Question?" Kelly wondered what it would be. They'd been together for hours already and Tiffany hadn't indicated there was any kind of question.

"Yes, Kelly. I wanted to know if you would do me the honor of becoming my maid of honor?"

Kelly smiled brightly and stood boldly

beside Tiffany. “I would be honored!” The two women hugged, and for a moment, both women felt something flutter within.

Kelly pulled away, thinking, “This is my brother’s fiancée!”

Tiffany shuddered, silently. “What was that?”

Neither woman discussed it, but just chalked it up to “sisterly love”…

The next day, Kelly agreed to meet Tiffany after work and head to the dress shops to find the perfect bridesmaid dresses. Tiffany had also asked her step-sister, Mandy, and a colleague, Yvette, to be bridesmaids. Together the four women entered “Sophia’s Bridal Boutique.” The place was pretty, yet simple, much like Tiffany. She wasn’t someone who liked fancy-shmancy items. Simple was perfect, every time.

As the girls began to try on the many choices, Tiffany entered one of the change rooms with Kelly to assist her in zipping up a stubborn zipper. Kelly smelled good. Her skin was soft. Tiffany thought about smacking herself. “What am I thinking? This is Chad’s sister!”

Kelly was enjoying Tiffany’s touch, but could barely resist the urge to let her know. Then, turning around to face

Tiffany, she asked, "How do I look?"

"Amazing!"

"You'll make a beautiful bride..."

"Thanks," she sighed.

"You're not having second thoughts, are you?" Kelly asked.

"No, nothing like that. Chad's a great guy!"

"Yes, he is..." Kelly agreed. "But do you love him?"

"Yes. I love him."

"Okay...but are you in love with him?"

"I don't know what you mean," Tiffany said.

"I mean...when you touch him or he touches you, do you get the urge to kiss him all over?"

"I..." Tiffany didn't know how to answer and looked painfully uncomfortable.

"I'm sorry Tiffany; I didn't mean to make you uncomfortable."

"It's okay...I'm just..."

Kelly hadn't let her finish her sentence before she uncontrollably grabbed Tiffany and kissed her passionately on the mouth. Though Tiffany was shocked at first, she soon found herself reciprocating the kiss. Then suddenly they pulled away from one another and gawked weirdly at one another.

"What did I just do?" Kelly gasped. "Oh Tiffany, I am so, so sorry!"

Kelly was about to run out the door

when Tiffany grabbed her arm. “Don’t run, Kelly. We both participated in that kiss...”

“What did we do?!” Kelly asked. “You’re my brother’s fiancée!”

“And you’re his sister!” Tiffany panicked. “I can’t believe I betrayed him like that!”

The girls were both speechless. Neither knew what to do next. Then Kelly said, “I already knew I was a lesbian. I have liked girls a long time, and I should have let my interest in you be secret.”

“This is new to me, Kelly, I admit that. Yet I have to admit, I felt something spark,” she said, “but I don’t want to hurt Chad!”

“Me either, Tiffany,” Kelly added. “I felt something too, but I will not betray my brother.”

As the two girls emerged from the change room, their faces displayed awkwardness.

“Everything okay?” asked Mandy.

“Yes,” replied Kelly, “just discussing some details about the upcoming nuptials.”

Tiffany felt terrible and really didn’t know what to do, but with the guilt bothering her deeply, she decided to call it a day. “Know what girls, I need to go lay down. I have a terrible headache.”

Without another word, she left the girls and drove away. Although the other girls didn't know what to make of it, Kelly understood. She too felt terrible.

A few days passed and the two girls avoided one another strategically. Although he didn't understand what had transpired between them, Chad had become concerned. So, in an effort to "work the case," he went to speak with Kelly privately.

"Hey Kell..."

"Yeah?"

"Can you be honest with me?"

"'Course!"

"Well...I noticed that you and Tiffany seem to be at odds, which seems weird to me. You were getting along well, then POOF...nothing?" He paused a moment and then continued. "Did she say if she was having second thoughts?"

"No Chad. Nothing like that, but I..."

"What?"

"It's nothing. She loves you," Kelly said.

"That's a good thing, right?"

"Yes, I guess. But I can love a Cocker Spaniel; that doesn't mean I'm in love with the dog."

"I don't get your meaning."

"Oh Chad, I wish I could take it back...but I can't."

"Can't take what back?"

Kelly's stomach churned like curdled cheese.

"Kelly? What did you do?"

"Oh Chad..." tears filled her eyes as the guilt and shame overwhelmed her.

"Heavens Kelly, just tell me. Nothing can be that bad! Can it?"

"I think maybe it can be," Kelly took a deep breath and finally blurted it out. "I kissed Tiffany!"

Suddenly, there was silence. Chad just looked at Kelly with complete dismay. He was crushed, hurt, enraged, and shocked. "So you lose a girlfriend in Atlanta and suddenly feel the need to hone in on my fiancée? Who does that?!"

"I'm sorry!" she cried. "I'm sincerely..." she grabbed for his arm, pleading for forgiveness.

"Get away from me!"

Enraged he jumped into his car and drove steadfastly to meet Tiffany at the zoo. When he found her, up to her elbows in elephant snot, he firmly said, "We need to talk! Now!"

"She told you, didn't she?"

Tiffany walked over to the cage wall and the two carried on the conversation through the holes. "Why didn't you tell me she put the moves on you? She shouldn't have done that. I am very sorry."

"Chad, I am the one who should say sorry."

"Why, she kissed you, right?"

"At first," she nodded, "but then..."

"You didn't actually kiss back, did you?"

"I did, but..."

"Tell me it was a mistake and that it didn't mean anything..."

"It was a mistake, but I'm sorry, it did mean something," she confessed.

"You're not in love with my sister, are you?"

"Chad, I do love you. I love you dearly," she began. "But I didn't know what love was until..."

The look on Chad's face was devastating. Tiffany's heart broke with his. He didn't say another word, but turned and began to walk away.

"Chad, don't go!" she begged.

Chad didn't even look back. He simply got back into his car and drove away.

Immediately, Tiffany called Kelly.

"Kelly..." she cried. Her voice was filled with pain.

"Chad was there, wasn't he?"

"Yes, Kelly, he was so hurt...he just took off!"

"I'm sorry, Tiffany," Kelly confessed. "I didn't mean to hurt you two."

"I need you to come to the zoo ASAP!"

"On my way!"

Chad drove his car to the top of the big hill and just sat there, staring and thinking. He felt incredibly betrayed. He cared for Tiffany deeply and loved his sister without question, but they'd fallen in love and now he was faced with the embarrassment of it all.

In the meantime, Kelly arrived at the zoo and was let into the clinic area to speak with Tiffany privately. Tiffany was washing up for the day and putting her things away, when Kelly entered.

"Tiff?"

"Hey, did you hear anything from Chad?"

"No, I was hoping you had."

"No, not a word," Tiff said.

"I want to ask you something before we do anything more about Chad."

"What Kelly?"

"Do you love Chad? Or do you love me?"

"Kelly, I do love your brother." Kelly looked disappointed, but then Tiffany said, "But I am in love with you. That kiss..."

"I know, I felt it too."

"I just never dreamed about hurting Chad," Tiffany said.

"I can't believe we did that to him!" Kelly said. "I don't think he'll ever forgive me."

"I might." Suddenly, they turned around and saw Chad standing behind them.

"Chad!" Kelly cried.

Tiffany stood silently.

"Chad, I'm..."

"Quiet, Kelly, I came to say something and I want you to hear me out!" The girls nodded and waited for a terrible lashing. "I have to admit, that was not the news I was looking to hear today. I was utterly shocked and hurt. Very confused."

"I'm soo..."

"Wait, I'm not finished," he blurted. "Kelly, all of my life I have loved you. You're a fantastic sister and I know you wouldn't hurt me deliberately. And Tiffany, I know you are a good person, you're simply not capable of hurting someone on purpose. The fact is, however, you both hurt me. But, it made me think. What possible reason could there be for you to both betray me in that manner. That's when I realized, you two were in love."

"What are you saying Chad?"

"Well Tiffany, I know you love me, but I can see that you are in love with my sister, and if that makes you both happy, then I want you to let it be."

Tiffany and Kelly could barely believe their ears.

"You're the best!" Kelly said, hugging her brother with all her might.

"You are an amazing guy." Tiffany didn't know what more to say, but gave him a gentle kiss on the cheek.

"Just promise me something," he said.

"Anything!" Kelly said.

"Name it," said Tiffany.

"Just be good to one another, okay?"

"Agreed!" they said.

As evening fell, Tiffany took Kelly back to her place and sat cozily with her upon the sectional sofa. Their passion was heating up and now they were free to be in love.

"I can't believe Chad," Kelly said.

"He is amazing, isn't he?"

"Hmm...and so are you, Tiffany."

Suddenly, without any further delay, their passion burst like a cannon ball and the two women began kissing one another with infatuated passion. Their lips melded together as their tongues slipped into the mouths, sensually enjoying the passions of a great French kiss.

Then carefully, Kelly began to move her hand down Tiffany's body and found her firm and delicate breasts. With a tender touch, she grasped a breast and carefully began massaging the nipple. Then carefully, she proceeded to move her hands beneath the smock and lifted it over Tiffany's head.

Tiffany then began to unbutton the blue blouse that Kelly had been wearing and carefully stroked the breasts as she passed them. Then with the last button finally unfastened, Tiffany removed Kelly's blouse, revealing the sweet brazier beneath.

Next, Kelly began to unfasten Tiffany's blue jeans and teasingly slipped her fingers past the soft pussy inside. Tiffany's body felt good with Kelly's delicate touch.

Then, Tiffany aided Kelly in removing the shorts she'd been wearing, revealing nothing but her panties.

Finally, Kelly removed Tiffany's denims and casually stroked the panty line as she slipped her fingers toward the clit.

Their lips continued to exchange passionately as the girls continued to stroke one another's breasts, purposefully fondling the pussy from time to time.

Then, with sensual passion, Kelly began to move her tongue toward Tiffany's pussy and gently moved the legs apart, followed by the tender pussy lips. Then with her tongue extended further, she began to teasingly stroke the clit, massaging it passively.

Every fiber of Tiffany's being began to tense and pant. Her heartbeat elevated as the goose bumps climbed her back excitedly.

With each groan and moan, Kelly intensely moved her tongue around the clit, focusing on the alluring g-spot. Tiffany's eyes reached far back into her head as her toes gripped deep into the fluffy carpet and her hands grabbed for the sofa cushions. Her cry finally leaped from her body as her orgasm released the climatic passion within. Her body felt so good, but she was not about to let Kelly go without.

Without any hesitation, Tiffany began to lick Kelly's clit. Kelly was already intensely aroused by the passion that had illuminated to this moment, and at the very impact of Tiffany's touch, her body began to arch firmly backward. Her cries were loud and intense. Tiffany found the g-spot perfectly and did not let up. The climax rose deep into the soul of Kelly's body as she finally screamed, "Oh God!" Her orgasm was intense and satisfying. Now lying on the sectional beside one another, the two women cuddled in the nude and just enjoyed getting to know one another all through the night.

The wedding was temporarily cancelled but was later replaced when Kelly and Tiffany wed. Their "I Do's" were sweet and sincere, and Chad proudly cheered them on as he toasted them at their wedding.

It was an unexpected vow twist, but he was glad they found one another, before he and Tiffany had said "I Do." Though Tiffany would not be his, he was glad to still have the two women he loved most in the world—next to his mother of course—in his life.

3 CIVILIZED LOVE

It was the 14th of July, just about three weeks after the Civil War ended. Now, battered and torn, Pvt. William Jacobs rode his faithful steed back to a land he once knew very well. Now he would return a stranger.

The bloodbath of Gettysburg would forever remain in his memory bank. The blood of his slain brother would be an image that would haunt him for all time, the blood of an adversary he'd always loved. John was his brother, two years older, and they'd always been close. John, however, had the same mindset as his father.

"We bought our slaves fairly! We paid full price for them. We aren't bad owners." that was their perception. William, however, never agreed. From the time he was a child, he had often played with the young black children, in secret. The one time he was caught, his father tanned his hide good.

Despite the many moments of lecture, William could simply not believe in owning another human being. Even though the common mindset placed the slave below a human's status, William knew in his heart it was different.

His mother, Caroline, didn't say one way or another what she believed. She was the wife and had to know her place. It was Caroline's sister, Margaret, who felt differently and often said so, to those who'd listened. Most folks just referred to her as the mindless spinster. Fact of the matter was she was the only woman willing to speak. That didn't sit well with most men. Yet William liked that about her. He'd often sit with her and talk, listening to the ramblings of the town's loon. Caroline barely spoke to Marg because she could not condone her meddling ways. Then, when war was declared and folks were called into battle, William took a stand for the North, walking away from his family's beliefs, for that which was right.

As the horse cantered through the entrance of Georgia, jarring the pain that still wracked his shoulder; his mind began to melt over the memory of the bloodiest battle he hoped to ever see. "Enough blood for a lifetime, or two," he thought. He'd been shot and left for dead, piled among the bloody carcasses of his friends and allies. The river beneath him ran red as the smell of rot and gunpowder competed with the summer's willowing breeze.

The final picture replayed in his mind, slow motion sounds muffled to the memory as the battle unfolded. If he thought hard enough, he could still hear the big bangs of the cannons as they rumbled like thunder through the valley.

They'd charge into battle, both sides, in the battle of all battles. There, in the midst of the Battle of Gettysburg, in Adams County, PA, North and South were to head in a bloody battle that took the lives of more than 7,000 men. As the dust settled and William was able to find his footing once again, he began to pull himself back to his people. The few who were left, thought to have been killed along with the rest, had almost left him entirely. As he came into view of his comrades, something caught his eye.

He'd walked over one corpse after another. He tried not to look. He tried not to let it sink in. He didn't want to think about the loss. He just wanted to go home. Now, a coat from the other side caught his attention among the thousands. It was

John.

William's blood turned cold within him as it left his face and dropped him to his knees. Looking upon the blood spattered body of his brother, he knew without a doubt that John was dead. William hung his head and cried. "What has hate brought to us, brother? What has it brought?" He sobbed and sobbed. His comrades heard the cries of a pitiful man and soon recognized their friend.

"William?" Dobs, one of his fellow privates, asked. "Why do you cry over this Confederate?"

"This... is my brother," William replied.

Dobs stood, silent, as William tried to stand. Then suddenly, in the shock of the aftermath and loss of blood, William collapsed. It was three days before he awoke in the hospital, lying beside the window of amputated body parts and in a room with those who were left to live with the memory of the momentous hill of slaughter.

Now, entering the gates of his father's plantation, he saw row after row of black folks walking, with few possessions. He smiled and nodded at the few he'd remembered. Their smiles were hesitant but sincere. He'd been one of the good guys, they'd concurred. Yet he was still a Jacobs.

As his horse neared the house, William could hear the voice of a very familiar soul shouting for glee. "William!"

William turned his head to see the bountiful aunt he'd always loved, running to him with open arms. Eager to see her, he quickly dismounted and embraced her with open arms. His shoulder hurt like hell, but it didn't matter. He was glad to have seen her first. It made coming back seem less awkward.

"Oh, dear boy!" She said, joyfully. "It sure is good to see you!"

"Good to see you, too, Auntie Marg."

"How are you doing? How's the shoulder?"

The family had been telegrammed with the news of both sons. John's death would, no doubt, cause a ruckus for William. His shoulder wound was minor compared to the pain he'd have to face with his parents.

"It's fine, Auntie, just fine."

As they got reacquainted, the door to the house opened and shut. He looked to the porch and saw his father standing there, staring him down with cold resentment. Unwilling to embrace his treacherous son, he left the porch and walked to the barn, shunning William's existence.

Still, William had to try.

Entering the house, his mama was quietly waiting for him at the bottom of the staircase. She wore a long, yellow dress with white lace. She looked old and smelled of booze. She stared at him as if she were staring at a stranger.

"Hi, Mama," William said. "I'm home."

She looked at him with wonder. "William..." That was all she said. She smiled, slightly. Then she heard the footsteps of her husband as he came up the porch.

The door opened and William turned around quickly. "Hello, father," he said.

"I am not your father," he said, sternly. "My only son was killed, fighting for our pride."

"Gerry!" Scolded his mother.

"You stay out of it!" He said, harshly.

"He was my son, too. Both of them are," she said.

"You remember whose side you're on!"

"Father, you can't treat her like that!"

"You...Yankee...You are NOT welcome in my home!"

"We can't turn away William!"

"You want to lay down with the slaves, you stay in their quarters and fend for your own feed. I wash my hands of ya!" His father began to turn and walk away. Then he said, "you best not be babying him, now. He's a traitor and the William you loved is dead to this family. You remember that good, woman!"

As Gerry stormed from the house, the room went silent. Margaret, who'd been outside, entered the house and frowned at her sister, "You ought to be ashamed of yourself, Caroline!" Then, with nurturing eyes, she looked at William and said, "Come, son. You can stay with me." Feeling the loss of his family, William agreed, and went with Margaret to stay.

After what felt like 20 years of sleep, William woke up feeling almost as young as he was before the war began. The house was quiet and bare. Then, stepping outside, he heard the bustle of the city and decided to board his horse. He rode through town until he found a small café restaurant that was serving a hearty Southern breakfast.

Entering the restaurant, first he'd been unnoticed. Then one of the fellows recognized him and sneered. "It's one of them damn Yanks!"

"Damn Yanks!" The people growled.

Feeling the daggers and coals of deathly eyes, William kept his cool and walked down until he found a table that was on its own. Then, as he sat down, he began to read the local paper. It talked of the war and the new life of the South. He was pleased, but it was keenly apparent that was not a shared view at this café.

As he read the paper, he heard a sweet voice say, "Coffee, sir?"

"Yes, please," he said, almost not looking up. Then he saw her hand. It was dark. He looked up quickly and smiled. "Denni?"

She looked confused. He'd recognized her.

"Do I know you?" She asked.

"It's me, William Jacobs," he replied.

"Oh, William, of course." She smiled with fond memory. They'd played together in the past. William had, in fact, been a friend of her brother, Sammy.

"How are you, Denni?" He asked.

"I'm good, William. How are you?"

"Good," he smiled. "Say, where's Sammy at? I should go say...." Suddenly, the look in her eyes caught him cold in his tracks.

Tears were in her eyes. "War got him," she sniffed softly, trying to hold back the tears.

"Oh, geeze Denni, I am so sorry," William's sincerity was real.

As he consoled Denni, a big fellow name Bud, who'd been listening nearby, spoke up and said, "Good, one less nigger!"

"Shut your mouth!" William scolded. "Not in front of the lady!"

"Lady? I don't see no lady," he groaned.

"Seriously, Bud, cool it. The war's over. She's free. Move on!"

"She may be free from slavery. Then again, she may be free for a good fuck, too, right?"

William was ticked and stood tall before Bud. "Listen Bud, I am asking you. Stop it. Now!"

"Or what?"

"Or, I will be laying some big, white Yankee kick ass all over your big, fat, ugly Southern one!"

Suddenly the room erupted with rage. The men charged William and began to kick and punch him viciously.

"Don't hurt him!" Denni cried. Then Bud, who heard her, turned quickly and slapped a tray of dishes from her hands. They tumbled noisily to the floor in one big crash.

"Now you're free to clean up that mess you made!"

Then the men grabbed William and began to drag him into the street. There they continued to kick and punch him, until suddenly the Sheriff fired a shot into the air.

"What in the world are you all doing?" He snapped, as they turned to look at him.

"This Yankee was causing trouble, Sherriff." They said.

"Really?" He replied. "And it takes 6 men to make him stop?"

"He's a nigger lover!"

"Listen boys, I'm from the South, too. I don't much like the changes, myself. But, the law is the law, blacks are free and the war is over. Beating on a Yank won't change that," he said. "I suggest you boys return to your activities and leave the Yank alone."

They didn't like the idea at all, but agreed, reluctantly, to return to the café.

Now, bleeding and sore, William lay on the ground and looked up at the Sherriff. "Thank you," he said weakly.

"Don't thank me, Yank. Had this been five years ago, I'd have let them hang you!" With that, the Sherriff left and returned to his office down the street.

"Here, let me help you," Denni said. She helped him to his feet and led him, and the horse, back to their tiny home. It was dark, gloomy, and full of holes. Yet in an instant, the family welcomed him inside.

They tended, carefully, to his wounds.

"Don't look like anything's broken," said Denni's mother. "You're lucky, boy."

"Thank you, Mum," he replied.

"You one of the good guys, I presume. We called to help you. It's the Lord's way," she explained.

Denni and her mother worked endlessly to help William's wounds mend quickly. They fed him what little they had. They mended his torn clothing and he returned the favors by reading to them from the Bible, and even attempted to teach them to read. Reading had been against the law.

Denni caught on quickly.

"You're doing amazing!" William said as she began to read a page from Shakespeare's "Hamlet."

"This book is amazing!" She said. "I didn't know stories like this existed."

"Oh, definitely. Why, at Margaret's there are so many books it would astound you!"

"I believe I'd like to see those someday," she said.

The twinkle in her deep, dark eyes tickled his heart. He smiled.

"What?" She said, seeing the look on his face.

"You're amazing!"

"You mean, with the books?"

"No. You. You're amazing!"

She blushed, feeling awkward.

His rugged good looks made her smile. Green eyes and light skin were not known, to her people as anything more than slave owners. William, however, was different.

"I don't know what to say," she said.

"Don't say anything..." He gently grabbed her face, pulled his lips to hers, and gave them a tender kiss.

She reciprocated the kiss but replied, "Careful... What will people think?"

"I don't care what people think. Never have!"

"That's true," she snickered. Then she looked at his scar and stroked it gently. "You got this for my freedom..."

"I know there are many roads ahead, yet. But we fight for what's right, no matter what the cost!"

"Like freedom, right?"

"And love..."

She got quiet. She'd had feelings for him for a while, now, but slapped herself for liking a white man. "It won't work," she told herself. She gulped. She didn't say anything more. Yet when he grabbed her shoulder and pulled her head until it touched his chest, she felt oddly at home.

They lay quietly and said nothing. He loved the way she smelled. Her fragrance was sweet and pure. Her skin was soft and supple. She listened to the beat of his heart and her own melted within. Her fingertips strolled gently over the scar on his shoulder. Then, she gently kissed it.

A few days later, William was feeling better and returned to live with Margaret. He sat quietly on the porch and drank his lemonade, his mind consumed with Denni. She was a beautiful woman. So what if the color of their skin was different. In a town like this, it could never be, and he knew it.

"Thinking about her, again, aren't you?" Marg asked as she stepped out upon the porch.

He silently nodded.

Margaret sat down beside him and said, "Love does not have a color, William."

"I know that, but this town would never accept us," he said. "They barely tolerate us now."

"Where love exists, there has to be a way," she said.

"I don't know, Auntie Marg. I just don't know," he sighed.

"You love her, don't you?"

He sighed, earnestly, "Yes...I do."

"Then, there will be a way!" She said. "You wait and see." She smiled as she walked back inside to finish making supper.

He continued to sit and think, as he recognized a figure approaching the front gate. She was dressed as pretty as a picture. Her dress was old, but it had been altered to fit her fine figure. Her jet-black hair had been slicked and curled into ringlets.

"Denni!" He exclaimed.

"Hi, William," she replied. "I know I am taking a chance being here, but I couldn't stay away one moment longer. I know I am crazy to feel anything for you. You're white, I'm a slave..."

"You're free!" He declared.

"Only by law. But, I am still in chains here," she declared.

He knew it was true.

"I have to get out of here!" She said. "I want to be where I can enjoy being free!"

"What do you mean?"

"North. I need to go North, to a place that recognizes me as a woman, not a freed slave." She said.

He sat, quietly.

"But, I won't go...if..." She seemed uneasy.

"If what?"

"Oh, William, I know I am crazy to ask this. It's not proper..."

"Ask what?"

She fumbled on her thoughts and looked incredibly uncomfortable.

"I might be crazy... But, I think I'm in love with you. Oh, that does sound crazy," she rambled. "I... I... If you tell me you don't love me, or that I am mad and crazy, then I will just go and let you be. But, if you feel the same for me..." Her body began to quiver as she struggled with her words and emotions.

William smiled and approached her slowly.

She looked like a terrified child. Her eyes were full of compressed tears as she composed what little dignity she had left. "I'm sorry William, it was silly for me to say..."

He gently placed his finger upon her lips. "Shh..." He said. "You don't have to say another word."

She stood agonizing over what he would say next.

"I love you, too," he said.

"We can't be together though, can we?"

"Not here," he sighed. "Maybe a change would do us well..."

"How will we do it? Where will we go?"

"I imagine a city like Chicago or New York would be best... Though I imagine a white man and black woman would still be odd," he confessed.

"Well, we can at least try, right?"

"We can," he agreed.

"We don't have much, but we'll make it, right?"

He smiled and hugged her, wanting to say, "Yes," but knowing it would be tough. Since his father had declared him dead, the inheritance was gone. There was nothing for him, nothing but his horse and bare essentials.

Margaret had been listening at the door. She smiled as she thought. "Oh, hi Denni," she said as she exited the door.

"Hello, Miss Margaret."

"You know, William, I was just thinking."

"Oh?"

"I was just thinking it was time for me to move away from here." She said.

"Move away?"

"Well, Mr. Jinkens did offer to buy this old place for a good price. Would be enough to finally get out of this town."

William was confused.

"You know, William, I got that mare and wagon. I won't need it. Could you use it?"

"What? I can't..."

"Buy it?" She asked.

"Well, yeah"

"You silly boy!" She scolded. "Don't you know by now how much you mean to me?"

"I guess I do."

"Boy, I'm getting on in years and want to live my days by the ocean, something small and quiet. You know, boy, I have your inheritance locked up, but I am thinking..." She winked. "I am thinking you could use it now, couldn't you?"

He was speechless. Denni offered a semi-smile.

"Tell you what. I am going to head South with what I need. You sell what I leave and it's yours!"

"What? No!" He gasped. "I can't let you do that!"

"It's what I want, William."

"You sure?"

"It's what I want. Please let an old lady have her way, okay?"

William didn't know what more to say. Margaret had always won her arguments. Instead, he simply hugged her, "I love you,

Aunt Marg."

"I love you, too, son."

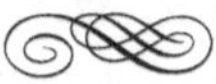

With Margaret heading South, and their wagon heading North, William and Denni were thrilled, and scared, about beginning lives anew. As dusk began to fall, William pulled the wagon to the side of the trodden road and set up a small shelter for the night.

"Are you nervous?" Denni asked.

"No. Well, maybe a little," William confessed.

"Me, too," she said. "But, in a good way."

Denni gazed dreamily into the fire and smiled warmly. Sure, life hadn't been easy, but she liked where it was heading.

In awe of her beauty, William sat closer. "You are so beautiful."

She smiled warmly as she looked into his eyes. "Oh, William..."

He leaned down to her lips and kissed them gently. Without hesitation, she returned the passion. Then, with lust growing in her body, she began to slide her fingers in between the buttons of his shirt and stroked his body, gently. He loved her touch; it made him swoon. Then, he kissed her again. This time the passion locked and they kissed with magical intensity.

He gently began to kiss her down her neck and she sighed softly with delight. He gently moved his fingers beneath her blouse and found his way beneath it, revealing the caramel tipped nipples, perked with excitement. He grabbed her gently as she moved her hand into his pants and loosened his buckle. As she unzipped his denims, she soon discovered his pleasure perked to attention.

His cock was bold and thrust. She continued to move her hands over him and helped him remove his shirt entirely. Then, she gently began to kiss his scar and moved her mouth downward until her lips slipped softly over his thickened penis. She gently sucked it, arousing him all the more.

She moved her hands to her waist and slipped off her petticoat and skirt. Now, with her legs, she moved her toes along his thighs. Then, she returned to kissing him on the mouth. He found her body to be perfect and gorgeous as he moved his hands over it, gently yet firmly.

With his body flexed, he moved his mouth down towards her pussy and gently parted the lips. With his tongue, he began to lick and tickle her clit. The arousal of his touch urged an energized moan of ecstasy. Her body flexed with excitement as her eyes rolled with euphoria. He continued to lick her emphatically and without mercy while he slipped his fingers into her vagina, elongating the moment of arousal.

As he slurped and tickled her clit again and again, her moans and cries peaked high into the night, until the climatic eruption released her of the fathomable pleasure. Her head spun with pleasure as he soon moved his cock into place. He increasingly moved his cock in and out of her dripping vagina, with pleasure for them both. Her body continued to grope his, while his cock took pleasure in the moistened vaginal opening. The tension that held his cock in place elevated the pleasure as he called out for glory and soon released the pearly white substance within his beauty.

Now panting with pleasing fatigue, they fell upon one another and covered themselves modestly beneath the starlit sky. She placed her head against his chest again and sighed with warmth from within.

"Oh God, you're amazing!" She said.

"You are, too, Denni," he replied. Then, thinking a little more, he had a thought. "I know this may seem crazy, but I want to ask you something."

"Anything," she said curiously.

"I don't know whether we will have any obstacles or not, but if you would do me the honor of becoming my wife, I would love the chance to marry you."

"Marry you?" She said with sweet surprise.

"Without reservation," he confirmed.

"Regardless of the obstacles we might face, I know I will love you, always, and I want to be with you always. Marry you... That is a definite yes!"

"I love you, Denni Jackson!" He said, as he grabbed her, again.

"I love you, too."

The night fell quiet as their love and passion continued to grow. With a journey still to unwind, the only thing they could be sure of was their love. Whatever would be would be, but nothing and nobody would tell them they would not be a couple. Their love would withstand all the battles of the civilized new world and would carry on for generations to come.

4 VINNY'S NIGHT CLUB

Kandi Driscoll began her shift at Vinny's Night Club for the first time. She was nervous, but was trying desperately not to show it. She had barely turned twenty when her family kicked her out of home; now she was forced to make it on her own. College had not been an option: it was simply not in the family budget. She managed to find a room for rent, but didn't mingle much with the other singles living in the home.

Initially she had gotten herself a job in a local coffee and doughnut shop working on a graveyard shift. She didn't mind the hours so much; it did provide a premium of a whole $1 per hour, but it was still tough going. As she poured her 100th cup of coffee for the day, she began to feel dread. “This fucking sucks. I work so damn hard and can barely make rent, much less buy groceries. How the hell am I going to survive?”

No sooner had she said that, Talia entered her coffee shop.

“I’ll have my coffee with one cream and three sugars, please,” she said. She squinted slightly and read the nametag. “Kandi….”

“Sure, I’ll get that for you right away!” Kandi smiled brightly.

Kandi immediately noticed how poised and glamorous Talia was. A tall Latin-American woman, in her late twenties, perhaps, but you couldn’t tell. Her skin was flawless and her smile was bright and beautiful. Her eyes were illuminating. Green and bold. She was well dressed and well presented. Nothing about her seemed “unusual.”

“You’re up late,” Kandi remarked. It was three in the morning and most people were either at work or in bed, so she was curious.

“Just got off from my shift,” she replied.

“Oh, where do you work?”

“Uh…,” Talia seemed resistant to say immediately.

“Hey, can’t be worse than working here!” she groaned. Then fearing she’d be in shit for saying something against her company, she recanted her statement somewhat. "I mean, this place is 'great'...," her tone was sarcastic and almost a little desperate.

"That bad, huh?" Talia asked.

"The job isn't so bad, but there's not much caching at the end of it."

"I know what that's like. I was doing something like this when I was about your age," she explained. "That's when I made my career change."

"Oh, what do you do now?"

"I ahh... I'm a dancer."

"A dancer?"

"Yes, at Vinny's."

"Oh... you mean a stripper?"

"Well, yes... but it's more than that. And it pays VERY well!"

"How well?" Kandi inquired. "If you don't mind me asking."

"I don't mind. It really depends on how good you are and how the clientele is on any particular night. On some nights, I make $200; on some nights, I make that in an hour," she explained.

"Holy shit!" Kandi gasped. "That sure beats this hell hole!"

"I'm sure it would." Talia looked Kandi over, in her very "non-flattering" garment, and looked at her pretty face. Although Kandi was terribly hidden by the polyester clothing, Talia could see the potential. "Well, you know Kandi...Vinny's looking for new talent," she paused. "Why not come to try out? I'll even put in a good word for you."

"Really?"

"Sure. I can tell you're pretty. Though that uniform doesn't leave much for the imagination," she said.

"No kidding. I feel like a clod in this getup!"

"Well, you have a nice figure and a pretty smile. With the right attire and some fancying up, you will look great, I can tell."

"Thanks," Kandi said. "So, when should I apply?"

"Why not come by tomorrow at about 5p.m.," Talia said. "I'll let Vinny know you're coming."

"I'll be there!"

Talia paid for her coffee and wished Kandi a good evening, wondering if the young girl would actually do it or not. It was Talia's experience that most girls talked themselves out of it a half a dozen times before making their decision to dance, or not.

The thoughts of making good money and surviving beyond the peanuts she was currently making seemed enticing. Yet, stripping was taboo in Kandi's family. What would her parents thing? She considered the idea throughout the evening and weighed the pros and cons. Then, with all things considered, she decided that she would "give it a try."

After a good "day's" sleep, Kandi awoke with a plethora of mixed feelings. Excited, nervous, and confused, but nonetheless she was prepared to make it work. Not knowing what to expect, she arrived at Vinny's Night Club and tapped upon the rear door.

A large bulky man answered the door and said, with a firm rasp, "State your business."

"Hi," she said, quivering silently. "I'm here to audition for Vinny's. He's expecting me, I think."

"Hold on!" he barked.

"The man is fucking huge!" she said quietly to herself.

She was right. Michael was appropriately nicknamed "Bulk." He was easily 6' 6" tall and about 300 pounds. His arms, neck, chest, and thighs were massive. They emphasized his existence. A few ever challenged him, for no one ever won. He was the bouncer: bold, mean, and intimidating to anyone who needed to be kept in place. Yet, when it came to the girls, he was nothing more than a big ol' softhearted teddy bear.

After a few moments of waiting, Bulk returned. "Name?"

"Kandi."

"Okay, Kandi, come on in. They're expecting you," he opened the door wider and let her step in, then shut it firmly behind him. "Hey, Kandi?"

"Yes?"

"Knock them dead." He winked and offered a tenderly warm smile.

She no longer felt afraid and returned the gestured smile, "Thanks!"

After a brief introduction and general "interview" chitchat with Vinny, Kandi was given the chance to change into something sexy so she could strut her stuff. She was terrified. In fact, her fear began to cause her stomach to churn, but then she shook it off and focused on the task at hand.

Kandi was incredibly gorgeous. Her youthful appeal was electrifying. Soft supple skin, fair yet sweet. She had long blonde hair that flowed lusciously down her back. Her legs were long and lean. Her eyes were electrically blue and were immediately captivating.

Suddenly, the music was ringing and the lights were flashing. The show of her life had begun.

The club had six poles, three cages, a large elevated dance floor, and multiple props to boot. Unsure of where to begin, she simply grabbed a pole and began to move around it as she danced to the music. Apprehensively at first, she could see that Vinny was less than enthused.

"You got more than that, don't ya? We want the men to drool here, Kandi."

Feeling the need for greed, she began to work that pole, working it for all she was worth. She groped it and straddled it. Then, she turned around and shook her booty boldly in Vinny's face. And what a booty it was.

Vinny was thrilled. "Oh the men will like her ass for sure!" he said. "Got some J-Lo ass going on here!"

Then, she teasingly turned her head, licked her lips, and stroked her long silk legs. Their youthful appeal was fully intact. Then, like a cat, she moved silkily along the floor, moving her ass and back up and down, dragging out each move with an enticing glare.

Then, she moved her body to face Vinny and playfully let her full "C" cup breasts swing gently in the black- and red-laced bra. Then sitting upward, she shook the straps and let the hooters have a little time in the jungle. Vinny raised a brow.

"Oh fuck me, baby!" he whispered to Talia. "This girl's hot!"

"Told ya!"

Then, standing to her feet, Kandi slipped the straps down around her shoulders and hinted that she was about to release the jugs for his viewing pleasure. Talia watched as well, fully impressed.

Finally, releasing her final thrust of enticement, she unhooked her bra and pulled it off briskly, letting the youthful breasts move freely in the gleaming lights.

Then, the music stopped.

There, in nothing but a tiny thong, Kandi stood, hoping this display was enough to get her the job. She sat nervously, holding her breasts fashionably, and waited.

Vinny turned to her and smiled. "Soooo...Kandi. When can you start?"

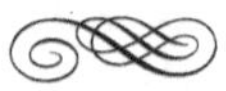

Kandi gave notice to the doughnut shop and was soon able to start at Vinny's. She showed up for her first shift and was as nervous as she had ever been in her life. She peeked through the curtain and could see hoards of men sitting in their tables, gawking for the show to begin.

"Nervous?"

Kandi turned around and saw a tall lanky girl towering over her. She was all dressed up with the sexiest props imaginable. And while she did appear to be fantastically attractive, the intense look in her eyes made Kandi shutter. Still, she kept the peace, given that it was her first night.

"I am," Kandi replied.

"I see," she looked Kandi up and down, checking out the cha-ching competition.

Sensing the trouble, Talia, who was about to join the group, intervened.

"Come on, Bambi...."

"Brandy!"

"Yeah, whatever. This girl is new and does not need your bullshit before hitting the stage for the first time."

"What's it to you, Talia?" Brandy sneered. "She's not your bitch, is she?"

Brandy—not so secretly—had a thing for Talia, but Talia would have nothing to do with Brandy. Yet, that didn't stop Brandy from working her stuff for Talia's attention.

"Nor are you Brandy."

"Come on, Talia. Look at us," she coaxed. "We're both smokin' hot and sizzle the stage every night. Imagine what we could do together!"

"Nothing's hot with you, Brandy. You're too fucking cold to be hot."

"Oooo," hissed the other girls.

"Okay ladies," said Rooster, the stage manager, preparing the girls for the show. "It's time to get your booties on!"

Then in a flash of dry ice, the eight ladies began their fabulous show of hooters and asses. The men in the audience howled and drooled accordingly.

The first three girls walked out and got the men going. Brandy and Ira went next, leaving Talia and Kandi in the wings, waiting for their cue.

"Oh God!" Kandi's gut was churning horribly and her body felt tense.

Talia, recognizing the fear, said, "Hey sugar, don't you stress it, baby. Just follow my lead."

Kandi nodded, and with a gesture from Rooster's hand, the two girls hit the pole in the center stage.

"Must be a new girl," said one of the regulars.

As all eyes were on Kandi, she gulped, but then, with Talia's expert leadership, she soon began to work it out. Her show was hot and flawless. She shook her cheeky ass pleasantly, her hooters engaged the wagging tongues of the men, and her sexy moves certainly got a rise for many cocks in the audience.

Talia and Kandi played off one another in such a seductive way that Vinny couldn't help but notice. Brandy noticed too.

Kandi wasn't necessarily a lesbian, nor was she necessarily straight. She simply hadn't found out one way or another. She wasn't a virgin, but until this night, she hadn't considered being in love with a woman. Yet, Talia was hot. Fucking hot!

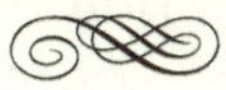

The show was flawless. It went off without a hitch and the men loved Kandi. She'd made her mark and Vinny was thrilled. Talia was equally thrilled. She'd discovered a natural!

"You did an amazing job!" Talia said.

"Not bad, huh?" Kandi pulled the wad of cash together and quickly counted it up. "$487!" she gasped.

"That's great for your first night!"

"I didn't make $487 in a week at the shop," she couldn't believe it. "I could get used to this."

"Good, cause you're a natural," Talia said.

"Well, I was nervous!"

"We all get that way. And sometimes that doesn't change, but it's the rush that I do it for."

"Not the money?"

"Hmm...Yeah, that too!"

"Well, I think this could be a great start for me," Kandi said.

"No doubt," Talia said. "Now, I just need to go speak with Vinny, then we will be hitting the showers. Get all this glowing goop off of me."

"Okay," said Kandi. Then, grabbing a towel and robe, she made her way to the showers by herself. The showers were open and had six heads to shower from. Kandi placed her shampoo, conditioner, and soap upon the ledge and then began the water. As the water began to run warm, Brandy entered the room.

"Soooo." she said.

"Hi Brandy," Kandi replied.

"Movin' in on Talia, are ya?"

"Wasn't moving in on anyone. I just came to work," Kandi said.

"You looked like you were really getting into the bitch when you were dancing."

"She was a great help up there."

"Listen here, bitch!" Brandy moved closer and looked her square in the eye. "The girl is mine. Get your own bitch, or I'll fucking gut you, got it?"

"Look, I'm just trying to wash up here so I can go home to my cat, okay?" Kandi replied.

"Get moving on then," Brandy snapped, "Then get the fuck out of here!"

"Brandy, I think it's time for you to go!" snapped Talia. "You're not for me and you are no longer for Vinny's Night Club."

"What do you mean?"

"You're fired!"

"You can't fire me!"

"Can to! Vinny just made me assistant manager: in charge of the dancers."

"You're full of shit, Talia!"

"Take it up with the boss, but we already discussed you, and you are gone!"

"I'll cut you, blonde! You cost me my job and my bitch!" Brandy screamed.

"Sounds to me like you did that on your own."

Suddenly, Brandy began to shriek like a mad woman, uttering her death threats so loudly that Bulk and Rooster came running. The shock of naked women didn't faze them—that wasn't new for them—but seeing Brandy with her hands around Kandi's and Talia's throats alarmed them.

Without hesitation, Bulk tazored the bitch and knocked her to the ground. Then, they cuffed her and dragged her sorry ass back to the office where she'd await the arresting officers.

Meantime, Talia and Kandi stood alone together in the shower. Kandi was still naked as could be, shivering and wet.

"Are you okay, honey?" Talia asked.

"Yeah, I'm fine. You?"

"Other than being pissed, I am fine."

"Did I cause a rift between you two?" Kandi asked.

"Hell no, sugar," Talia replied. "She's not my type."

"What is your type?"

Talia smiled seductively at Kandi. "Well, I don't know if you're straight or not, but you are a fine piece of woman!"

"Well, Talia," Kandi said, watching Talia undress for the shower. "You're a mighty fine woman yourself."

"You think so?"

"Definitely!"

Without further delay, Talia gently placed her palm upon Kandi's cheek and moved in for a sweet kiss. Kandi had no resistance. Talia was all she'd ever wanted in a partner. She just hadn't expected her passion would be a female. Male or female: it didn't matter. Passion is passion and love is love. The heart doesn't lie.

With the warm water flowing over their naked bodies, Talia began to lick down Kandi's neck and moved forward towards her pink and perky nipples. Then gently she began to suck upon the left nipple, making the sensual fascination run through her body.

Then, grabbing Kandi gently, she laid her down to the floor, where they proceeded to French kiss one another without catching their breaths. While they passionately shared this kiss, both women moved their fingers along their partner's body, sending erotic waves of heat through their bodies, pulsating the excitement they were feeling in their vaginas.

Kandi was receptive to every touch and followed Talia's tender lead. Then, Talia gently began to stroke the surface of the clitoris and Kandi reciprocated the same touch with Talia's clit, allowing gentle and loving sensual strokes of pleasure.

The intensity continued to rise as the climactic euphoria moved through their bodies. With eyes rolling back so far and toes and hands gripping firmly, the very peak was reached with moans and cries of grateful orgasmic release.

With their bodies fondly aroused and released, Kandi could barely believe how wonderful her life was becoming. Her family had kicked her out to tend for herself with a peanut-paying job and little to survive on.

Now she sat cozying with a fantastic woman, partner, and boss. Their sex and passion would only increase as the dollars continued to roll in. From coffee cup to silver pole—Kandi couldn't have planned it better.

5 WHITE GLOVES

Daniel Patrick Carter, aka Danny, stared sorrowfully out his new apartment window, wishing he had had a better relationship with his father, Jim. Daniel had been dealing with his "gayness" for some time now, but Jim would not have his son "shame him." Anytime Danny showed sign of being gay—or weakness as his father called it—he would meet the wrath of his father's hand.

"I'll beat that faggot-bullshit curse out of you yet, boy!" he'd say, often with some kind of thrashing. "I have two kids: a daughter and a son! Not two daughters."

While Danny's mother Jean didn't care that he was gay, she never spoke up. She didn't want to face the wrath of Jim either.

Jim didn't respect Jean at all. She was his wife and he was the man of the house. Whatever he said or decided was how things were to be. She learned early not to question it.

Jenny, his twin sister, on the other hand, was uniquely strong. She didn't mind her father one way or the other. She was strong enough to stand up to him, and for some reason she was the one person in his life he didn't thrash on.

Still, she had no respect for him. She didn't respect her mother either. "Leave him!" she'd tell her. She never could understand why Jean would allow him to dictate and beat her, just taking it. Despite all of the abuse she took from Jim, she time and time again would defend him against anyone who'd say he was anything but wonderful.

The people knew. The cops had been called to their home a number of times. Medical reports claimed suspicion, but no charges were ever filed. Jean would simply lie about the bruises, but Jenny and Danny knew the truth.

Jenny and Danny were close, as close as two siblings could be. Jenny knew he was gay and she couldn't have cared less. She loved her brother and only wanted him to be happy. Then, when they turned 21, she insisted they begin lives of their own—away from their father's backhand.

Finally, he'd come to the decision of moving out. Jim was not approving.

"You can't move out boy!" Jim said. "Not a sissy boy like you..."

Despite his disapproval, Danny finally made the move to be out on his own. And while he knew it would be terribly difficult to survive financially, he was happy for the trade-off. Jim was a great provider. Money was never an issue. The kids had always had the best of the best for food, clothing, and more. But for Danny, it wasn't about money; it was about dignity and self-respect. Both of these were in short supply in the Carter household.

Now, Danny was a fine-looking man—small, but very attractive. He stood only about 5' 6" and weighed no more than 100 pounds. He was quite athletic. His Bowflex machine had been used religiously and it showed. He had gorgeous dark hair, brown eyes, and a golden brown complexion; undeniably, he was visibly appealing.

Jenny had moved to Cambridge to attend University, but because she loved her brother so much, she texted him several times a day.

Danny had taken some classes to become a pastry chef. He was good at it, fantastic, in fact. His father couldn't stand knowing his son was a "pastry" chef. He'd tell his friends that he was the executive chef in a fine dining establishment, but the fact was that, while Danny was a great cook, his talents lived in deserts and pastries.

Now out on his own, Danny began his own bakery business specializing in cupcakes. His passion for fine "tastries" was evident with each mouthful and his business was booming.

Danny had had a rough start in life, with the negative back lashings from his father, but he was on his way to bigger and better things. Yet, "coming out" was still in progress.

William Goldberg was an openly gay male nurse. He didn't care what people thought. By the time he was in his mid-teens, those who surrounded his life were well aware of his sexual orientation. And although it was awkward for his family to accept at first, they soon let William be the man he was intended to be.

As an effective male nurse, William worked primarily on the ICU wing, providing around-the-clock care to patients with serious injuries or illnesses. He's seen many things in his profession, and he had little time or patience to entertain those who would discriminate for their own lack of moral character.

While he was a sinfully handsome nurse, the women knew he was off bounds. He wore his gay essence on his sleeve, but for the most part nobody cared. He was a fine person, a caring and attentive nurse, and an avid friend. There wasn't much William wouldn't do to help someone in trouble. The women who worked on the floor felt comfortable enough to entrust him with their secrets. He was honest and kind.

The patients loved William, especially the children. He would talk to the patients with compassion, without patronizing them. From the prick of a needle, to the bathing, to the changing of bandages, William took care to make the patient as comfortable as possible.

For the coma patients and for those who sat with their loved ones, he'd offer a good listening ear and an attentive heart. He'd encourage them to be strong and let them have a moment of weakness. This nurse was nothing short of amazing.

William was one of 3 gay nurses on the floor, yet he was not drawn to either of the men he worked with. Ted was quite a bit older and preparing to retire and had been with his partner for 27 years. Filipe was a nice enough guy, but they shared few interests. Though they did go out to dinner a few times, both agreed to keep their relationship professional.

William was tall, about 6’ 2”, and had an average weight. He was a talented gymnast, having competed many times in his youth. As an adult, he maintained his athleticism by practicing his routines daily. His biggest talent revolved around the rings and pommel horse. His biceps were formed accordingly. He had soft blonde hair and bright blue eyes.

It was now Thanksgiving and Danny and Jenny had gathered at their parents’ mansion to enjoy the fine turkey dinner Jean had prepared. While it was being prepped in the kitchen, Jim settled down upon his lazy boy recliner to watch the game. He was on his fifth beer by the time Danny arrived.

“Come watch the game boy!” he insisted.

“I think I will give mom a hand in the kitchen,” he replied.

“Fucking sissy boy, the kitchen is for women!”

“Dad, I’m a chef.”

“Not a chef, you’re a dough boy,” he scoffed. “You like cooking so much, why not become a real chef?”

“Not now Jim.” Jean scoffed. “It’s Thanksgiving!”

“Get back in that kitchen and fix

dinner. Mind your own damn business!"

"Dad, quit it!" Jenny said. "We're trying to have a good dinner here and you're ruining it."

"Keep your nose out of this, Jenny. I'm talking to your faggot brother here."

"He's not a fag dad! But he is gay. Get over it!"

"I do not have to get over it and he will not be gay when I'm done with him!"

"Dad, stop it now or you're going to die miserable and alone!" Jenny had reached the breaking point.

"Oh, really, Jenny?" he scorned. He got up from his chair and stormed out of the room, not saying another word.

"Wish he'd just quit his bullshit!" Jenny said.

"He's never going to accept me being gay." Danny said.

Then, Jim returned to the room. "Jean, get out here!" he shouted.

Without hesitation, she left the kitchen and entered the living room area. "Yes dear?" she asked.

"It's your fault my son is a faggot!" he shouted.

"Jim!" she scolded. "Don't...please..."

"Your fucking cunt deprived me of a real son!" Then without any further notice, he held out his 44 magnum and fired a shot into Jean's head. She fell dead.

"Mama!" cried Jenny.

"What'd you do!" Danny asked, screaming at his father.

"You're next faggot boy!" Then Jim turned the gun towards Danny and fired the shot, but simultaneously; Jenny pushed Danny out of the line of fire. The bullet hit Danny's arm, but missed the chest Jim had been aiming for.

"Jenny!" Jim scolded. "How dare you!" Then he fired two shots at Jenny, hitting her in the stomach and head. She fell hard.

Then aiming for Danny again, Jim fired the gun again, but it did not fire. Enraged Jim charged at Danny and hit him across the head with the gun. Danny was out cold.

After a few moments, Danny came to, but was immediately alarmed when he realized the house was on fire. He was dazed, but forced himself awake. He looked at his mother, but he knew she was dead. His father was nowhere to be seen. Then he crawled to Jenny's side. She was breathing.

"Oh thank God!" he said.

Then with all the strength he had in him—ignoring the pain of his arm and head—he carefully dragged his sister outside. As he exited the house, three neighbors ran over.

"What happened?" asked one neighbor.

"My father!" Danny said. "He tried to kill

us! He killed my mother!"

"Holy shit!" gasped the neighbor.

A second neighbor had already called the fire department, but immediately informed them of the violent crime that had occurred.

"Where's your dad now?"

"I don't know." Danny said, "The car's gone."

Jim was gone and Jenny was fighting for her life. Danny prayed for a miracle "God, don't let her die!"

After several excruciating hours, Jenny was moved into the ICU. The bullet that entered her back had severed her spinal cord; Jenny would never walk again. They safely removed the bullet from her brain but she still remained in a coma. Now only time would tell what the outcome would be. Doctors specified that the next 48 hours would be critical. Danny was crushed.

As quiet settled around the chaos and pain, Danny sat at his sister's side, holding her hand and encouraging her to fight. Then William walked in the room.

"Hello sir," he said. "I'm William. I will be Jennifer's nurse for the next twelve hours."

Danny acknowledged with a slight nod,

but he was tired. A bandage was placed upon his head and his arm was set in sling.

William completed his patient assessment. He checked her vital signs and made sure his patient was comfortable. Danny sat quietly. William knew the dynamics of the case and couldn't imagine the pain Danny was in.

"Sir…" William said. "Is there anything I can do for you?"

"No thanks, William," he said. "Just make sure my sister's alright."

"Of course I will. Listen, I am going to be here with her all night, so if you'd like to get some sleep or…"

"I'm not leaving Jenny."

"Okay sir," William said.

"You can call me Danny."

"Sure…Danny."

For the first thirty minutes, neither man said much. Yet, William continued with his job. There were two patients in his room, and he was fully attentive to them both. The woman in the bed beside them had been in a serious crash and she too was in a coma.

After some time passed, Danny began to open up. "William?"

"Yes Danny?"

"Whatever you do, don't let my sister die!"

"Danny, we will do everything possible,

but I know your sister's going to feel your presence and want to fight. So it's good that you're here."

"I won't be going anywhere until she's out of danger!"

"I understand."

Danny eventually got a few hours of sleep in his chair and the day rolled over to the next. William had gone home but returned punctually for his next shift. Then, once he'd checked Jenny's vital signs, he grabbed a large paper bag he'd brought in with him.

"Hey, Danny," he said, "I brought you a few things."

"What is it?"

"I don't know, just some stuff."

Danny opened the bag and looked inside. He found a pair of clean sweats, a T-shirt, clean socks, and a packaged pair of underwear, as well as some toiletry items for washing.

"Oh gee, thanks William." he smiled. "How'd you know?"

"Been doing this a long time!"

"Well, thanks."

"You're welcome."

Danny entered the restroom adjoined to the hospital room and got the much-needed shower he'd been longing for. Fresh and clean, he felt renewed.

Danny finally reemerged, feeling utterly new, at least physically. The scars of the deadly event were still reminiscing in his mind. He couldn't escape the images that haunted each time he closed his eyes. As he opened the door, he saw two police officers waiting with Will.

Danny had a feeling he knew what they were there for, "Is this about my father?" he asked.

"Yes sir, it is."

Danny didn't know if he wanted to know, still he waited for them to finish.

"I'm afraid your father's body was found an hour ago," explained one officer. "He'd apparently driven his car off the Main Street Bridge. Shortly after..."

"I see." Danny said. He felt indifferent about it. He didn't know whether to be relieved, angry, or sad. Fact of the matter was, he felt all the above.

"I'm terribly sorry, Danny," William said after the officers left.

"I'm alright," he said. "At least he can't hurt us anymore." He began thinking about his mother. "I guess I should be planning my mother's funeral too," he sighed. "I just don't know how to be here for Jen and deal with that too."

"It's alright," William said. "We managed to contact your aunt Judy. She'll be here tomorrow to help with anything you need."

"Oh shit, that's great!" Danny said, with a sigh of relief. "She'll know what to do."

With relief in sight, Danny was able to

sit back and focus on Jenny and their futures. He'd managed to close his shop for a few days, with a sign on the door, but missed baking.

"In the meantime, I have some good news for you," William said.

"Oh?" Danny inquired.

"Well, we were checking Jenny's vitals while you were in the shower, and she most definitely shows signs of improving. In fact, her vitals are maintaining their own, and I expect she will be opening her eyes to see you any day now."

"Really?!"

"Yes Danny, really."

"Oh thank God!" Danny leaped towards William and gave him the biggest hug of his life. Then suddenly, the floodgates of woe and joy burst through like a damn and Danny could barely control his emotions. His heart was overwhelmed and the tears flooded crazily. He just clung to William and cried.

William just let him let go. He patiently waited for Danny's overwhelming release to run its course.

Then finally, as he regained his composure, Danny released his grip from William. Suddenly, he felt embarrassed.

"Oh man..." he said, "I'm sorry."

"Don't worry about it Danny," William replied, "You needed a good cry!"

Danny smiled. "Thank you so much

William! You've been great!"

Jenny's color was returning, but she still lay quiet in her bed. She was out of any immediate danger, and Danny was starting to regain his appetite. Then, William's shift replacement arrived for duty.

"Listen, Danny, Amber is going to take my place for the next 12 hours," he said. "I will be back tomorrow."

"Okay." Danny paused. As William gave Amber the updates of Jenny's condition, Danny sat and held her hand. "Jenny, don't you worry about anything. You just come back to me, okay. We're safe now. I just need you to come back to me."

"Alright Danny, I'm off. I'll see you tomorrow," William said.

"Wait!" Danny blurted.

"What's wrong?"

"Nothing..." Suddenly Danny became aware of his awkwardness. "I was just thinking."

William smiled. "About what?"

"Well, I was wondering if you'd be interested in having some dinner with me?" Danny asked. "I'm starved!"

William smiled again. "Yes Danny, I'd like to have dinner with you."

"Great!" Danny looked back at Jenny and hoped she'd be okay.

"It's alright Danny, she's in good hands."

"Alright then, let's go."

Danny and William walked down to the cafeteria, but the natural cook inside Danny quivered with fear. "Oh God!" he gasped. "This just won't do!"

"What do you have in mind?"

"Know what?" he said. "I've been dying to cook something. Let me take you to my place. I'll cook us a fantastic meal!"

"Oh, you cook?"

"Sure do. Ever heard of 'DP's Bakery?'"

"Sure have, great treats there!"

"Well, it's my shop!"

"You're DP?"

"Yes sir."

"Fantastic!" William said.

When they reached Danny's apartment, he immediately began to pull together a fantastic homemade meal. He made some fresh pasta with the most fabulous Alfredo sauce in the world. Then he created a fantastic soufflé for dessert. William felt spoiled.

"Dinner was fucking amazing!" William boasted.

"My way of saying thanks."

"Just doing my job."

"Oh William, I know lots of nurses. You're exceptional and I wanted you to know it."

William smiled modestly accepting the compliment and then said, "Danny, can I ask you something?"

"Sure?"

"Are you seeing anyone? I mean, correct me for assuming, but are you gay?"

"Wish I wasn't."

"Why?" William asked.

"It's what caused my father to do what he did..."

"Danny, your being gay isn't the cause. It's your father's biases. Had he gotten to know what a wonderful person you were..."

"He never even tried."

"Some won't I'm afraid," William said.

"How long have you known?"

"Most of my life, I guess. By the time I was 16, I knew."

"I guess I did too, but wasn't allowed to talk about it. He'd get downright nuts if the subject came up."

"I'm sorry for that Danny," William said.

"It's not your fault."

"I know, but I do know that this prejudice exists."

For the next hour, the two men shared so many thoughts and feelings. They talked about their passions, their goals, the hobbies, and more. Without a doubt there was something clicking here.

Then, with little reservation, William leaned over to kiss Danny gently. Danny was a little shocked at first, but quickly received the passion and reciprocated the kiss.

With only a moment of hesitation, both men soon embraced with a passionate French kiss. Then like ravenous animals, they began to peel off one another's shirts. William lovingly began to kiss down Danny's neck and slipped his fingers gently through his gorgeous hair.

Then he gently moved his hands down to his pants, while Danny began to nibble on William's ear. Danny moved his fingers into the scrubs pants and began to loosen the tie that held them up. William moved his hand towards the cotton sweats he'd lent Danny and began to encourage them to move down his hips.

With some repositioning, both men were able to remove their pants, leaving their boxer briefs only. Both men were pleasantly erected, with cocks tenting sharply in their drawers.

Then with total fascination, William laid Danny back while he proceeded to embrace his cock with his mouth. With joyful sucking, William continued to suck the cock thoroughly. Danny had never had a man give him a blowjob before, but he was sure this would not be the last. William was so fucking hot; Danny couldn't believe he was so lucky to have him in his life.

As William continued to suck it, the tension ecstasy erupted into his mouth secreting the frothy, salty semen. Then without further reservation, Danny made way for William's cock to fully penetrate his anus.

With a singular, gentle motion, the cock made its way inside and then William began to rock his position over and over. First beginning with long deep stroke, but soon increasing with a larger sense of pleasure.

His eyes rolled around as the pleasure made him groan and moan. With the cock moving in and out, faster and faster, he finally erupted with pleasure and the two men collapsed with sweet release.

"You're amazing, William."

"You are too, Danny," William said. "Despite the challenges you've faced, you've become a fantastic man and I am glad to have the chance to know you."

"I feel the same way."

After five days of intimate growth and passion, the two men had unanimously fallen in love. Now sitting at his sister's side, Danny feels her handgrip. "William!" he gasped. "Look!"

William immediately took notice. "Jenny?" he whispered softly. "Jenny, can you hear us?"

"Come on Jenny...It's me, Danny. I'm here for you!"

For a moment her eyes flickered and fluttered, but then finally opened. She was dazed and moderately confused, but smiled immediately when she saw Danny.

"Oh Jenny!" he cried. "It's so good to see you!"

"I love you, Danny," she said.

"Love you too sis."

Jenny looked around the room and began to juggle the thoughts in her head. She hadn't suffered any memory loss. Danny, glad to see his sister's recovery in progress, said, "Jenny, I want you to meet a very wonderful person. This is William. He's been your nurse for a while now, and well, he's wonderful."

Jenny immediately noticed the passion between them and smiled. Although her recovery would be lengthy, she would be in good hands with her brother and his new lover—William, the nurse.

Pain had hit their family hard, but was replaced with promises and hope. Despite the criticisms and prejudices of their father, Jenny and William continued on a road of truth and determination. Regardless of the odds, they would certainly overcome, as long as they were on each other's side.

6 THE BIGGER PICTURE

David and Carl had been best friends since fifth grade and often enjoyed hanging out together. After a busy day at work, the two men had decided to unwind at Kristy's Lounge—a nightclub with beautiful, sexy women dancing while they enjoyed their beer and wings.

Carl is a straight man. Straight as they come it seemed, always gawking when a beautiful woman passed by. "Did you see the hooters on that dame," he'd say as he lastingly drooled. "Yeah, wanna get me a piece of that, huh?" Legs, breasts, and asses, he liked them all.

Now at Kristy's, Carl was howling like a ravenous dog. Trixie and Darla were his favorite dancers. Plenty of ass and titties to keep his tongue a wagging and his cock a tingling. "Fuck me baby!" he'd shout. The women got use to him. He was there a lot, it seemed. Shouting and drooling, but he was a good tipper and didn't get too inappropriate. The bow-wow calls were typical in this line of work and Carl didn't miss a beat.

As Trixie brushed by Carl's lap, with her tenderly soft, yet firm ass, she shifted it teasingly. This caused a tingling stir beneath the zipper of his Levis. She passed by Dave's lap too, but the response was quite different.

Dave was sweet and quiet. Never said much at all. In fact, he was often a gentleman.

"Hey man, what's wrong with you?" Carl would ask. "Don't you wanna piece of that delicious ass?"

"Sure," he replied. The fact of the matter, however, was that Dave didn't have the same sensation for women that Carl did. They didn't stir him at all. Jamie, the bartender, however did catch his eye. Yet, knowing how Carl felt about gays, Dave never let on.

Trixie and Darla moved across Carl's path again, waving their lusciously, perky breasts in front of his face. "Look don't touch" were the rules. But oh, did he want to get a hand full. Better yet a big ol' mouth full would be nice too. Darla turned her ass around and began to shake it teasingly at Dave, but Dave just smiled.

Carl kept shoving twenty-dollar bills into their panty straps and wishing he could finger more than that. Dave did place a bit of money in the straps, but his action was meant for show.

Carl had a serious boner going on and would have loved to have a frolic in the field with either woman. In the perfect dream, he would have been happy to have a two-fer. Oh, but it was just a dream. Carl had never had a serious relationship. He wasn't interested in settling down. Frolicking and fucking was all he cared about. The moment a girl got serious, he'd end it. Dave often told Carl that he was burning his bridges, but Carl would just say, "I have plenty of time to settle down. Let me enjoy my bull-hood while I am still young."

They were both still fairly young, twenty-two years old, working at the Hobart plant on a daily basis. Carl was a solid young man, husky and strong. He stood only about 5'9" tall, but he was handsome enough. He had dark brown eyes, short dark brown—almost black hair, and a gorgeous brown tan. The girls liked him, most of the time. Looks wise, the girls would drool, but he could be a bit of a pig at times, especially with a few beers in him.

Dave, on the other hand, was about six

feet tall, slim build, light brown and curly hair. He had gorgeous green eyes and a stunning smile. He was always a gentleman. His mother had taught him that. In his heart, he knew he was gay, but he simply did not want to let the world know it.

There were plenty of women interested in dating Dave, yet he rarely went out. A few times, he double dated with Carl, but when it came time to make out, Dave would simply say, "he didn't want to rush things..." Most girls liked him for that.

Carl, on the other hand, if a woman was ready to put out, then he was ready to serve.

Now, after a long night of drinking and gawking at Kristy's Lounge, Dave and Carl left for home. Carl was stupid drunk, but Dave had remained sober. Someone had to drive, he figured. As Carl staggered and waivered, Dave propped his friend into the passenger side seat and fastened him in. Carl barely spoke three words before he passed out.

"Finally, some quiet!" Dave said. He shook his head and then proceeded to the driver's side of the car. As he proceeded to open the door, Trixie began to approach.

"Hi there," she said. Her bright smile, gorgeous long blonde hair and sexy curves would have interested any man. "Mind giving me a lift?"

"Umm, sure." he replied. "Where you heading?"

"Well, I'd come home with you, if you wanted," she said with a smile.

"You're a nice girl Trixie, but I don't think that's going to happen, ok?"

She frowned. "Don't you want me?"

Dave hesitated.

"Your passed out buddy there would."

"In a heartbeat!" he replied. "But then again, he only likes girls for fucking."

"What's wrong with fucking?"

"Nothing." Dave said. "But I don't do 'one night stands'. That's Carl's thing."

"You looking to get hitched?"

"Maybe, if I find the right person."

"Aw, that's sweet," she forgave his brush off. "Well, if you don't mind sir…"

"Dave," he said.

"Alright, Dave," she continued, "if you don't mind, I could still use a ride to Coulter and 5th."

"Sure, get in."

As Carl continued to snore and drool, Dave kindly drove the beautiful dancer to the entrance of her Coulter Street apartments and dropped her off. After which, he took Carl back to his apartment and helped him into bed. Tired and worn, Dave opted to take the couch instead of driving to his own place. As he drifted off to sleep, he found his mind wondering back to James at the bar. "Now that's a babe!"

It was about 2 o'clock in the afternoon when Carl, in his hung-over stupor, wandered out from his bedroom. The sun was bright and immediately sucker punched him in the head. "Oh!" he moaned. "Where's the fucking Tylenol?"

Not realizing Dave was still there, he jumped when he heard Dave say "In the cupboard, as usual."

"Shit, Dave!" he gasped. "You scared the hell out of me!"

"Sorry man."

"It's alright," Carl said. "Hey, did you stay the night?"

"I did. After hauling your drunken ass to bed, I decided to sleep here on the couch. Just too tired to make it home."

"Yeah, that's fine."

Dave sat upon the couch with nothing more than a clean white towel wrapped around his waist. His clothes were still in the dryer. Although it was Carl's apartment, it wasn't unlike either of them to make themselves at home. They'd been friends far too long to worry about formalities. If you needed a drink, you simply helped yourself. Mi casa su casa.

Carl poured himself a much-needed cup of coffee and sat down upon the couch.

"Oh hey," he began, "Mom and dad want me to drop by in about an hour. Would you like to come?"

"Sure," Dave said. "Always liked your family."

"Apparently, Matt and Suzy will be there too. Don't know what it's about though."

"Ah, but no one needs a reason to see their family, do they?"

"Right."

About an hour later, they arrived at the Charter home, and his family was openly glad to see that Dave had come too.

"Hey man!" Matt said. "Good to see you!"

"Nice to see you too, Matt," Dave replied.

Matt was Carl's older brother. Older by three years. Suzy was their sister, and she was two years younger than Carl. Dave had been a friend of Carl's for so long that the family had practically adopted him as a member of their family.

Suzy was a pretty girl, looked a lot like Carl, only feminine. Many times over, Carl tried to set the two of them up. He'd have loved Dave to be his brother-in-law. He knew Dave was a good man and would take good care of his sister. Yet, Dave never really seemed interested.

"She's too much like a sister," Dave would say. That was his excuse, but it wasn't the exact truth.

Suzy was there with Jonathan, her boyfriend of two years. She looked very happy and John looked nervous. Dave smiled.

“I bet I know what the family thing’s for?” he said quietly to Carl.

“What?” Carl asked, cluelessly.

“I am betting there’s an engagement announcement about to be made!”

“You think so?”

“Hmm...” he paused. “I think it’s a good bet.”

Just then, Jerry, Carl’s dad, began to ting his beer bottle with a fork. “Okay everyone, we have an announcement to make here.” he began.

Immediately, the family gathered around, anticipating the BIG news. John and Suzy stood close together with a wistfully delightful look upon their faces.

“Last evening, this fine young man came to me with a question,” Jerry said. “It seems he’s in love with Suzy and wanted my permission to marry her. I said no,” he giggled. “Well, okay, I didn’t say no, but it was hard to believe that my little girl was going to leave me for another man. It is with pride and bitter-sweet joy that I announce to you all the engagement of Suzy and Jonathan!”

The family cheered and clapped with excitement. “To the bride and groom!” Matthew toasted.

"Here! Here!" they replied.

Then, teasingly, Carl elbowed Dave and said, "Guess you missed your chance, hey Dave?"

"Guess I did."

Then, coming forward, Matthew interrupted the celebration. "Family, I wanted to talk to you, but it's been hard finding a moment when we were all together. I know this is Suzy and Jonathan's moment, but I didn't want to miss this chance to tell you all something I think may be important."

Carol, his mother, looked worried. "It's nothing serious is it?" she asked.

"No mother, nothing serious," he replied, "just something significant."

"Okay Matthew, what is it?"

"There's no easy way to say this..." he paused.

"Just say it son." Jerry said.

"Alright." he said as he exhaled with fearful reservation. "While I have known it for years, I have never fully disclosed this to you."

"What didn't you tell us Matthew?" Suzy asked, offering her big brother support.

"Well...I'm gay." He paused immediately and said nothing more. Jerry and Carl's faces both dropped with shock.

"Oh, I knew that!" said Carol.

"What?" Matthew asked. "How did you know?"

"Shoot boy, I'm your mother."

"But you never let on."

"I didn't want to force the issue. I figured you were sorting it out for yourself and that when you were ready, you'd tell us."

"Really?"

"Aw Matty, I suspected it too," said Suzy.

"Really? How long?"

"Geesh Matty, I'm a girl and I have a lot of really good-looking girlfriends. You never took notice of them. Not even Tracy."

"Oooo Tracy!" Carl drooled. "I noticed her!"

"Of course, you did. You're as straight as they come, everyone knows you like girls! But Matty never showed that kind of reaction."

Carl was stunned. "How come I didn't notice? Did you enjoy watching the swimsuit models down at the beach that summer?"

"No bro," he said. "Well, not those models. I did enjoy watching the photographer though."

"Oh yuck!" Carl said. "I cannot believe my brother's a fag!"

"Hey! Watch it!" Suzy said. "That's Matty you're talking about."

"Matilda you mean." Carl replied. "Matthew...I mean Matilda...You fucking got to be kidding. You? A fag? Really?"

"Carl, try to understand..." Matthew tried to get Carl to listen, but Carl was too much of a homophobe.

"Dave are you getting this bullshit?"

"I uh..." Dave didn't know what to say. He was happy to hear that Matty had had enough balls to come out with his sexuality, but Dave could not bring himself to do it. In fact, in seeing Carl's reaction, he was even less "ready" to come out.

"Come on." Carl said. "I'm out of here." He insisted. "Suzy, I am sorry if that fag ruined your party, but I have got to get out of here!"

"Carl, you're not being fair!" she said.

"I can't deal with this shit!" Carl bitched. "Dad, are you okay with this?"

"Well, I must say, I am shocked, but then again, maybe not."

"Did you know dad?"

"No, not really." Jerry replied. "Though thinking back to all those sporting events and his lack of interest. Then watching him cozy with your sister's friends to watch Mama Mia."

"Oh God!" Carl gasped. "You really are a faggot!"

Dave felt awful. He didn't want to leave with Carl. He was embarrassed by his actions, but he left anyways, hoping that Carl would eventually come around.

"Hey Dave, let's go get some titties

tonight. I need some straightening up."

"Carl," Dave said. "I've known you for about 15 years now, and I have never seen you be so mean to Matthew. I mean, I know you got into it with him on occasion, but this…this is way over the top!"

"Dave. you're not seriously taking his side, are you?"

"This isn't about taking sides; it's about accepting him for who he is."

"Who he is is a Sheila, a pansy boy, a fucking faggot!"

"And he's still your brother," Dave insisted.

"I thought he was my brother, didn't know I had two sisters."

"You don't have two sisters, you have a sister who is marrying a man, and you have a brother who just happens to be gay. Not by choice, but by fact."

"Listen Dave, this conversation's going nowhere. I'm going to drop you off at your place and head to the tittie bar myself."

"Forget about dropping me off then Carl, I'll walk from here!"

Dave waited for Carl to pull the car over and then stepped out and slammed the door. "When you're ready to apologize for being an ass, you'll know where to find me!"

"Fat chance on that!" Carl screamed the tires angrily as he sped away, leaving Dave in a cloud of stinking tire burn and exhaust.

"Ass hole!" Dave shouted as he flipped him the bird.

Dave was still walking down Williamsburg Lane, when the long blue Lincoln pulled up beside him. The two honks of the horn caught his attention. As he turned, he noticed it was Matthew. Matthew pulled the car over and rolled down the window.

"Out for a stroll are you?" Matty asked.

"Not exactly," Dave said.

"Did Carl leave you out here?"

Dave nodded.

"Little shit!" Matty groaned. "Get in, I'll take you home."

Dave agreed and got into the car.

"Listen, I'm sorry if I caused any problems between you and Carl," Matthew said.

"You didn't," Dave said. "He did that on his own."

"Carl can be a bit stubborn at times," Matty said.

"Yep, I noticed."

"Where'd he go anyways?"

"Kristy's."

"Oh," Matty said. "And you didn't want to join him?"

Dave shook his head no. "Not my thing,

really."

"I didn't think so," Matty said.

"Really?"

"Really," he replied. "Listen, since you left before we ate, would you let me take you to dinner?"

Dave suddenly felt happy and scared all at the same time. "Umm, alright."

Matthew looked a little like Carl, the dark hair, eyes, and skin, but he was taller and thinner, a very attractive man. Dave had noticed before, but now—all of a sudden—he wasn't looking at Matty like a big brother any more.

Matthew took Dave to the "Blueberry Mountain" restaurant. It was a fine dining establishment with elegant music, beautiful décor, and a high-scale menu. Not Carl's cup of tea. His idea of fine dining usually consisted of about half a cup of grease and a napkin instead of his sleeve.

They sat down by the fireplace and listened fondly to the violinists solo.

"This is very nice," Dave said.

"It is, isn't it?" Matty asked. "I've been here a few times. Can't help but bring you here."

Dave looked at Matthew curiously. It had been eating at him since he heard Matthew's announcement. "Hey Matt, can I ask you something?"

"Sure..."

"When did you know?"

"What? That I was gay?"

"Yeah."

"I guess I've always 'known it', but it's only been in the last few years that I have accepted it."

"It took a lot of guts to 'come out' like that."

"I practiced that speech a dozen times at least."

"Seems like your mother and sister are cool with it," Dave said.

"Amazingly so!"

"Your dad."

"He's accepting it, but I know he was uneasy about it."

"Then…there's Carl."

"I knew he'd be weirded out, but I didn't know he'd completely flip," Matthew said. "I hate that this has come between us."

"Being gay isn't the problem Matt, it's his attitude about it."

Matthew looked sad.

"Listen," Dave said, touching Matthew's hand. "What you did today took a lot of guts, and you know Carl loves you. You're his big brother! You've always looked out for him. It might just take him a bit to get used to."

"I hope so."

"I know so!"

Suddenly, they were caught up in each other's gaze. Something had sparked, but

Dave was not about to "say it" out loud.

Then, after a delicious five-course meal, Matty drove Dave home.

"Do you want to come up?" Dave asked.

Matthew paused for a moment and then nodded his head.

Dave's place was spotless, clean as a whistle. A far cry from Carl's bachelor pad.

"Wine?" Dave asked.

"Sure," replied Matty.

Then, while Dave was pouring them the glasses of wine, Matthew stepped out upon the balcony and looked down upon the small city. The night was warm and pleasant. Air was clean and fresh. The sky was clear of clouds and full of stars. Perfect.

"Nice night, isn't it?" Dave asked.

"Yes Dave, it is," he agreed.

Then Dave, struggling to control his feelings, handed the glass to Matty and gently rubbed his shoulder. Matty turned and smiled.

"You're a terrific man Dave," Matty said.

"You're the amazing one!" Dave boasted. "A fireman! Risking his life for others. All I do is push metal parts into a machine."

"Nothing wrong with working hard, at any time."

"Well, anyways, I am proud of you," Dave said.

"You know Dave," Matty began, "for years I looked at you as a little brother, but in the last few years, I..." he began to quiver with fear. Dave hadn't come out. Matthew suspected it, but didn't want to push it.

"Matty, I've liked you a long time too." Dave admitted. "I've just found it hard to admit my..."

"The hardest sentence I ever said was 'I'm Gay'," Matty admitted, "but once I said it...ah...it just...it was like a weight was lifted off my shoulders and I was finally able to just be me."

"Really?"

"Really!" Matty confirmed. "I knew people would react indifferently. They always will. But like all 'differences' in society, it takes a while for some to accept diversity as being 'okay', and then again, some will never accept it. You just have to be strong enough to be true to you."

Dave looked down upon the city and watched as the lights at the corner changed from red to green, trying to wrap his head around the truth he'd been denying himself. "You know something Matty?"

"What's that Dave?"

"If I was going to be honest with myself and others, it would have to start with two sentences."

"Oh? And what are they?"

"First, I'm gay. That's right world, I, David Arnold Dryfuss, am gay! There I said it!"

"Feeling better?"

"Hmm…maybe a little."

"And the other sentence Dave?"

Dave turned around and looked at Matty square in the eye. "Carl wanted me to be his brother-in-law since high school, always trying to hook me up with Suzy, but that was never the sibling I had feelings for."

Matt looked at him with simple admiration. "So then?"

"It's you. It's always, for as long as I can remember, it's been you for a long, long time." David gulped. "There, now it's out," Dave said to himself. "Now what?"

Matty stood there just staring, "What did Dave just say?" he wondered. "Did I hear him right?"

Suddenly, they were both speechless.

Then finally, after a few moments of awkwardness, Dave continued speaking. "I'm sorry Matt. I guess I should have kept qui…"

Suddenly, without any more reservation, Matthew grabbed Dave's face gently and passionately began to kiss him. "I have felt the same way about you too!"

Finally, the gloves were off and love was in the air. Moving back into the apartment, Dave began to unbutton Matthew's coral dress shirt, while Matthew moved his hands into Dave's blue polo shirt. They groped each other's body with intense passion and lust. Their lips continued to lock, slipping their tongues in and out of one another's mouth. The passion and heat continued to rise as they continued removing one another's clothing. Then with tenderness and erotic passion, Matthew began to move his lips down Dave's body and formed a good seal around his stiffened cock.

Dave stood there, fully aroused, as Matthew continued to suck the cock with all his love, while his hands gripped the well-formed ass cheeks in his hand. Dave's free hands moved through Matthew's hair and held him firmly in place as the euphoria erupted the cum within, exploding with gusto into Matthew's mouth. Then without any hesitation, Matthew spun Dave around and carefully positioned his buttocks for penetration. Realizing that Dave's ass had not yet been tampered with, he entered with care. While it was initially a little uncomfortable for Dave, he soon found the pleasure of the solid cock's movement. Matty continued to rock his cock front to back, increasing the stroke's speed and depth. With each thrust of his penis, Dave found himself deeply aroused, and enjoyed every moment until Matthew's erected cock released its frothy foam into his anus.

Finally, with the release of both of their infatuations, Dave turned to face Matty again. At first, they just looked into one another's eyes, feeling the passions of their hearts pounding for one another.

"That was amazing!" Matty said.

"Very."

"I had no idea...all this time that you cared for me like that," Matty confessed. "I've loved you for years, just never got the nerve to say so, until now."

Dave smiled warmly.

"Dave, I do love you. I love you very much!"

"I love you too," Dave said.

Then as the night of passion melted to day, they'd lovingly pleasured one another several times over and now sat together at the breakfast tables, wearing nothing more than bathrobes. While they were enjoying their morning cup of coffee, they were suddenly surprised to hear the door open.

With no warning, Carl walked in. He stopped cold in his tracks when he saw Dave and Matthew in their undressed attire.

"What the fuck!" he gasped.

"Carl!" Matthew replied.

Carl looked at both of them and said, "Please tell me this is NOT what it looks like!"

"Carl," Dave said. "I have to be honest

with you man. I..." he gulped, fearing the reaction he knew would follow. "Carl, I'm gay. There, I said it!"

"What the fuck?!" Carl shouted. "My brother and best friend are fudge packers?"

"Carl! Stop being such a prick!" Matthew said firmly.

"I can't believe you're doing this to me!"

"No one is doing anything to you," Dave said. "Fact is, your brother and I love each other. We have for a long time and we're just now figuring it out. I thought you'd be happy that I loved your sibling."

"Suzy! Not Matt!"

"What difference does it make to you, who I love?" Dave asked. "It does not change the friendship we've had all these years. Nor does it change the fact that Matty is still your big brother who would do anything for you."

"This is retarded!"

"Carl, you know I love you!" Matthew said. "Why can't you just be happy for us?"

Carl just shook his hands and threw his hands into the air. "I just don't....arr..." He turned towards the door and began to open it.

"Carl, wait." Dave pleaded. "If our friendship means anything to you and if your love for your brother means anything to you, then you'd be happy to know that we found happiness in each other."

Carl leaned against the apartment door—slightly open, caught between his thoughts and feelings. He wanted to leave, but knew that he did love both of those men. He'd always love them.

So, closing the door and turning back around to face them, he took a deep breath. His eyes focused on two of the most important people in his life. How could he just walk away?

"So, you two really do love one another?" Carl asked.

"Yes Carl, we do," Matthew said.

"And this is for real? Not some kind of wild fantasy?"

"Carl, trust me." Dave said. "I love Matty. I have for a long, long time."

Carl took a moment to think about things and put his feelings in check. Then getting a better look at the big picture, he began to see the obvious connection these two men shared, he smiled.

"I guess I get to have my best friend as a brother-in-law someday after all, huh?"

"I anticipate that is a definite probability," said Matthew.

"Without a doubt," confirmed Dave.

"Well then, Dave," Carl said, giving his head a final shake, "welcome to the family!"

Carl embraced the two men and surrendered his prejudices for their sakes.

He loved them too much to let his own ego get in the way and from thereon offered his support and love. While he would need to find another man to go to Kristy's with, he was happy to know that Dave and Matthew were going to be happy together.

7 TAYLOR'S MAKEOVER

From the time Taylor Thompson entered school, she had been the endless target of tease and ridicule—the punch line to most kid's jokes, the victim of the meanest pranks around. Yet, despite her awkwardness, she never let it get to her much. Taylor stood about five foot, seven inches tall and had a great figure. Not that you'd ever know it by the smocks and rags she wore.

"Hey Taylor, the sixties just called. They want their moo moos back!"

"Hey Taylor, do you own a hairbrush? If not, I am sure my horse would share his!"

The cruel jokes even went so far as to humiliate her. A group of kids had planned on Jamie, a handsome boy, to ask her to a dance. When he did finally ask her, she was thrilled. She said, "Yes," just in time for the whole class to laugh at her.

"Go with you?" Jamie taunted. "Hell, I'd rather bring my dog to the dance... and he's a massive, drooly thing!"

She went home in tears.

There were kids that didn't tease her but, for fear of their own ridicule, they simply didn't get involved.

By the time they reached college, she'd hoped things would have improved. Yet they didn't. The cheerleaders and jocks, other desirables, made her life hell on a regular basis. Despite her struggle with people, she excelled intellectually. She had a solid 3.8 average, excelling in the major academics.

While she continued to focus on her schoolwork, Adam Garcia was struggling to keep his spot on the basketball team. He'd struggled with his grades all through school. Had it not been for his incredible athletic ability, he wouldn't have made it to Penn State at all. Fortunately, he got a scholarship to play on the basketball team. He was ruggedly fit and lusciously handsome, with dark brown hair, dark brown eyes, and masculine Latin features. He made the girls drool, but Amanda was his girl.

Amanda was a gorgeous blonde cheerleader. She was tall and thin with big blue eyes, a super white smile, and a kick-ass body. She stood out among the masses. It seemed only befitting that she was seen with Adam. They were the perfect 'Ken and Barbie' couple.

One day, Adam's coach, Coach Williams, pulled him aside and met with him in Dean Francis's office.

"Adam, you're an amazing athlete, boy!"

"Thank you, sir!"

"Hmm. Well, despite your amazing athleticism, you are flunking miserably. I fear we are going to have to terminate your scholarship if we can't get your grades up."

"Coach! You can't let them do that!"

"Son, you have to fix your grades, or we will not be renewing your contract for the next semester," Dean Francis emphasized.

Adam was crushed. He confided in Amanda, seeking a way to pull his grades up.

"I can't lose this scholarship!" he groaned.

"What ya gonna do?"

"I need a tutor," he admitted. "I have to have a tutor!"

"Who do you have in mind?"

"I don't know. Who do we know that's smart and hasn't got a life outside of their books?"

They looked at one another with a mutual look of response.

"Taylor!" they agreed.

At first, she was reluctant to help the bully jock. However, with a little pleading and persuasion, she couldn't turn him down.

"Fine. I'll do it," she said. "Be at my dorm Mondays and Thursdays at 4. Bring your books and I will help you."

"Thank you, Taylor," he said.

"Yeah, thanks for saving my baby," Amanda said, as she clung to her boyfriend's arm.

Amanda was glad that Taylor would be Adam's tutor. She was smart and ugly. A great match! She didn't have to worry about him falling for that bow-wow!

Taylor had made all the preparations possible to ensure Adam's best chances of getting better grades. Then, on the first Monday at four o'clock sharp, there was a knock at the door. She casually opened the door and welcomed Adam into her dorm.

"Welcome," she said.

"Thanks," he said, as he took a look around. Her room was neat and tidy. A few family photos hung on the wall and a framed photo of her on her horse, Medallion, sat upon her end table. Adam, also being a fan of horses, took note.

"Your horse?" he asked.

"Yep, that's my Medallion, a champion jumper."

"She's beautiful," he admitted. "You must miss her."

"Terribly."

"I have a horse too," Adam admitted.

"Really?"

"Yep. Buddy's his name," Adam said. "A solid four-time champion thoroughbred."

"Nice," she beamed.

He'd never seen her smile before. Her eyes sparkled beneath the thickened glasses. Her pearly white smile was almost alluring.

He shuttered. "What the hell?" he asked himself. "This is Taylor. Snap out of it!" He'd noticed something different about her which almost made her likeable, and it weirded him out.

The initial tutoring session went really well. She helped him learn how to learn. She didn't hold his hand but made him work for it. Her methods astounded him and he began to absorb what she was showing him. He was impressed.

On Tuesday morning, Amanda saw Taylor at school and decided to approach. "So, how'd he do?" she asked.

"Who, Adam?"

"Of course Adam, ditz!"

"Don't call me ditz!" snapped Taylor. "If you want to know how he did, ask him yourself. I am not going to share any of that information with you."

"Listen, bitch! You best remember your place, or I will put you back in it so fast you won't know what fucking hit you! Got it?"

"Whatever!" Taylor turned and began to walk away.

Angered by her attitude, Amanda grabbed Taylor's bag, quickly jerking her back. Taylor lost her footing and fell. As she fell, Adam ran up and scolded Amanda.

"Why'd you do that?"

"She forgot her place!"

"Her place?" he replied. "Her place is helping me pass this semester, so I can keep attending this school; her place is being left alone by you. Your place is leaving her alone."

"You're sticking up for her?" she asked. "Why? Look at her!"

"Amanda...," he groaned, "get over yourself and shut the hell up!"

Amanda was pissed. With an opened palm, she coarsely slapped Adam across the left cheek, leaving a handprint.

Taylor felt embarrassed.

"You didn't have to do that," she said.

"Do what?"

"Stand up for me," she replied. "I've dealt with Amanda all my life."

"You don't deserve it," he said.

Taylor smiled awkwardly. "Thanks."

"My pleasure."

Thursday afternoon rolled around and Adam found himself looking forward to his tutoring session once again. Amanda had forgiven him for the way he spoke to her, but she still had a dislike of Taylor's very existence.

"I can't stand him being with her!" she told Rebecca, one of her closest 'bitch in the house' friends. Amanda was popular, but only to a point. People used her and she used people. Whether she liked you or not, if she believed you would increase her popularity, she would invite you into her world. If, however, you were an undesirable, she'd do all she could to ruin you.

"I wouldn't worry about her," Rebecca said. "Adam won't get involved with that barf bag!"

"Yeah, but he seems to like her," Amanda said.

"Maybe on a 'student meets teacher' level," Rebecca suggested. "But I don't think there's anything beyond that."

"I expect you're right."

Adam arrived at Taylor's room at 3:55. He didn't want to keep her waiting. Still kicking himself for liking her at all, he wanted to be nice. After all, she was doing him a huge favor!

"Hi, Adam!" she said, with a smile, as she opened the door.

"Hi," he said, as he stepped inside.

Taylor was wearing a pair of shorts and a flattering pink T-shirt. Her hair was pulled up into a messy bun, and her glasses were sitting on the end table nearby. He was amazed. She looked really nice!

Nervous, he didn't say anything initially, but prepared for his next lesson with Taylor Thompson. As she reached for her thick-framed glasses, he grabbed her hand. "Don't put them on," he said, warmly.

"What do you mean?" she asked.

"Your eyes are so pretty. Don't cover them up."

"I can't see anything without them," she said.

He sighed, "You look nice tonight."

"I do?"

"You do," he acknowledged. "Why do you hide yourself? You have so much beauty. People just have to see it!"

"You think so?"

"I know so, Taylor," he smiled.

She blushed.

"Tell you what. Tomorrow after school, I am taking you shopping. We are going to get you some contacts and your hair done. Maybe, even, something new to wear!" he claimed.

"Why would you do that?"

"My way of thanking you for helping me?"

She felt awkward and hoped it wasn't some sort of mean setup. "I don't know..." She paused.

"Please, Taylor. I'd really like to do this for you," he pleaded.

"Four o'clock?" she asked hesitantly.

"Four o'clock. I'll pick you up out front, okay?"

She agreed. Her heart skipped a beat. Adam, one of the hottest boys in school, was taking her out. Sure, it wasn't a date. Sure, it was probably some sort of charity act, but she didn't mind. Maybe she had a friend finally. The thought made her smile.

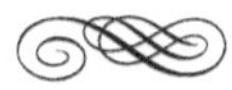

"What do you mean you're taking the barfy broad out?" snapped Amanda.

"I mean I am taking her out, Amanda!" he snapped. "And don't call her barf. She's actually a pretty good person when you get to know her."

"So what? She's a bad crack, a negative fixture for your reputation. You really want to be seen with her?"

"Right now, I would rather be seen with her than you!"

"Fuck'n asshole!" she sneered.

She tossed her hair hastily and stormed off in a huff. "Fucking loser. He better not fuck with me! I will make him pay!" Then she smiled sinisterly. "Better yet, maybe I will make her pay!"

At four o'clock, Taylor met Adam at the front of her dorm's building and was thrilled when he opened the door of his car to let her in. Amanda, who was several yards away, saw this activity and grew with contempt. "Adam! You son of a bitch!" she screamed. Yet being so far away, neither Adam nor Taylor heard her scream, but the people nearby sure noticed.

"Damn it!" said one boy. "Amanda's about to lose it!"

"All hell's going to break loose now!" said another.

At the mall, Adam took Taylor to an eyeglass shop and helped her pick out a pair of temporary new glasses that suited her face nicely while she waited for her contacts. Then, wanting to make her feel appreciated, he bought her a meal at the food court. It wasn't at all fancy, but it did make Taylor feel special.

Once he'd bought her meal, they went to a hairstylist, where she sat and had her hair trimmed, tinted, and straightened to a voluptuous shine.

While she was having her hair and nails pampered, Adam went and picked up a few flattering outfits for her to wear. By the time he returned to the salon, he was impressed! She was beautiful!

"Wow!" he said. Even though the scrubby clothing still hid her feminine figure, she was looking really nice. Then, composing himself, he said, "Here, I got these for you."

He handed her a bag with a pair of cute shorts and a tank top. She wanted to continue with the makeover, so she slipped into the ladies room where she tried them on. When she exited the restroom, Adam could barely stand it. Taylor was hot!

Though the contacts would have to wait, Taylor's transformation had been a success. "You sure do look beautiful," he said warmly.

"You think so?"

"Yes, I do," he smiled. He gently placed his hand upon her face and moved his face in to give her a kiss on the cheek. Then, happy to kiss her more, he moved to her lusciously sweet lips.

"Adam Garcia!" shouted a familiar voice.

"What are you doing?" She stormed as she approached. Then, while she stood there firmly, she looked Taylor over. "This cannot be Taylor!" she snapped.

"Yes, this is Taylor," Adam said.

"What the fuck are you doing?"

"I'm breaking up with you for starters!" he said.

Taylor stood there with amazement.

"Breaking up with me?" Amanda snapped. "You're not breaking up with me!" Then she turned her attention to Taylor. "You think a new look will change the barf bag we both know you are?"

"That's enough!" Adam said. Then, gently, he took Taylor by the hand and began to walk away.

Amanda was furious as Taylor and Adam walked away.

As they were walking away, Rebecca approached Amanda with caution. With the fury of vengeance in her eyes, Amanda declared, "You wait and see Rebecca! They will not get away with this! They will not!"

Taylor was a little rattled by the display of emotions and was quite unsure of what to expect next. Then, as Adam opened the door to his car to let her in, he asked, "You okay?"

"Yes, I'm fine. But I just made you

break up with your girlfriend," she replied.

"No, Taylor, you didn't do anything wrong. Amanda's always been a bitch, but it took knowing you to see what it's like to know a real woman!"

Taylor blushed.

Sitting in the car, Adam leaned over and gave Taylor another kiss. This time the passion was reciprocated and Taylor was beginning to allow her heart to feel what she'd denied for so long.

"Can we go somewhere quiet?" she asked.

"Sure. What did you have in mind?"

"Borden's Bridge?"

Borden's Bridge was a well-known 'hang out' for college kids to have sex at. This request surprised Adam. "Borden's Bridge?"

"Uh, huh," she replied. "If you're interested."

"I'm interested, Taylor! I am definitely interested!"

As Adam turned off the car and put it in park, Taylor began to release the woman she had within. Though she'd never done it before, she did not have any reservation. She leaned over and began to kiss Adam passionately. She slid her tongue into his mouth and the two tangled one another's taste buds intently. While they were locked in a tasteful embrace, Taylor began to move her fingers up under his shirt. For the first time in her life, she got to feel what great pecs and abs were all about.

The strong, smooth surface made her skin tingle with pleasure. Then, as she lifted his shirt over his head, she began to move her tongue down the length of his chest and torso. He began to slide his fingers through her new glossy hair and pulled her face back up to his. Then he gently placed his hands under her tank top and moved his hands toward her perfectly perked breasts.

As he placed the cup of his hands around each breast, his sense of arousal began to climb. The ugly duckling he'd once viewed as an outcast soon became the subject of his passion. He proceeded to lift her shirt over her head and tossed it into the back seat. Then he carefully unfastened her black brazier and flung it behind him, thus releasing her glorious white breasts. Her breasts were smooth and firm. The nipples were sensual, sweet, and pink.

Gently, he placed his lips around the left nipple and began to tickle it with the tip of his tongue. While his mouth was busy with the breast, his free hand moved toward her silky smooth thighs. He grasped the inner thigh and moved his hand smoothly up toward the opening of her shorts. Carefully, he slithered his fingertips inside. She sighed with excitement as the fluid began to tingle at her clit.

He moved his fingers toward the button of her shorts and gently undid it. He then proceeded to unzip the shorts down to the bottom. In the meantime she moved, increasingly gripping his shoulders with passionate arousal.

As he began to slither his tongue down her slender waist, he made her body tingle with pleasure. Goose bumps surfaced across her body as the other nipple became perky and firm.

Her panting increased with each stroke of his tongue.

Then, gently, he moved enough to lead her into the back seat, where he laid her gently upon her back. Without wasting any more time, he helped Taylor out of her shorts, revealing the black panties beneath. He wriggled his fingers gently along her clit and her eyes rolled back in ecstasy.

Her back arched as he gently moved his mouth toward the clit and delicately began to slither his tongue before moving it inside her, triggering her G-spot's sensual arousal. He continued to lick her pussy and clit while his fingers gently massaged the lips below. They were warm and moist.

Carefully he slipped out of his pants and loosened the tightened tent beneath them. Carefully, he covered his hardened cock with a condom, then continued to lick and fondle the beauty's moistened vagina. She moaned and arched with increased excitement, arousing his penis to a moistened peak.

Then, gently, he climbed upon her and inserted his cock. She moaned and flinched a bit as his cock penetrated the entrance and proceeded to move in with pleasure. With each stroke she panted more, and his body could scarcely resist the sensation.

He stroked and stroked, sending Taylor's eyes straight to the back of her head. Her body arched as she cried, "Oh, God! Oh, God!"

With a moan and whimsical cry of sheer delight and ecstasy, Taylor had met her climax and, while he completed a few more thrusts of pleasure for himself, the moment of release came for Adam, releasing the lava flow of salt-white cum.

With both of them lying naked upon one another, he could barely believe the scenario that had unfolded. His awkward tutor had become a phenomenal interest in his life. He was hooked.

"You know something, Taylor?" he asked.

"What's that, Adam?" she asked, with her hair draped loosely behind her.

"You're the most incredible girl I've ever known."

"I can't believe I'm here," she said. "This is like a dream."

"Well, if this is a dream, don't wake me up. I like being here with you," he said.

"I like it, too."

Though Amanda was less than impressed with the situation, she did not get a chance to enact her revenge. When Monday morning came, Taylor walked the halls with her piercing bright eyes and a confident stride, now hooked to Adam's arm.

When people realized how amazing Taylor was beneath the scuffed exterior, they no longer needed to exile her. Anyone from that day on who did would answer to her jock boyfriend, Adam.

Tutoring for Adam was never the same again, and walking the halls was never the same for Taylor, which was just fine with them both.

8 SHOVELS IN THE SAND

Lauren Smith's family moved into the high societal neighborhood when she was just about five years old. Her father John had worked exceptionally hard at making a financially successful business and was finally able to pull his family out of the projects and into a more "suitable" community. He was proud to have given them a clean and bright place to live in an elaborate neighborhood. Shara, her mother, was a teacher.

There weren't many black families in their community, but they fit in just fine, for the most part anyways. There were always a few idiots around who didn't get the memo that freedom was for everyone, but nonetheless, the family was happy in their new home.

Their neighbors on the right were the Borden family. They too had also had a five-year-old girl, named Shelley.

Lauren's family was warmly greeted by the Borden's, who welcomed them to the neighborhood and subsequently invited them for a barbeque dinner. Ava was known for her community hospitality. She was a domestic engineer and took the care of her home and family seriously. Her house was immaculate. Jason, her husband, was a litigation attorney who was sensationally successful.

As they socialized after the barbeque, they left Lauren and Shelley playing in the sandbox while the shared a bottle of wine. Lauren and Shelley clicked immediately. They built many sandcastles and clubhouses together. From the time they hit kindergarten until eleventh grade, they'd been inseparable.

Then, in the summer before 12th grade started, Shelley's parents were killed in an automobile accident. And although she would be set for life financially, she was still quite young and alone. Without a moment's hesitation, the Smiths invited Shelley to live with them.

Throughout high school, Lauren stayed away from boys. She wasn't interested in the dating life; she wanted to focus on her career. Her fascination with buildings led her to a passion for architecture. Shelley, on the other hand, met Robert in 12th grade. He was handsome, charming, and seemingly confident.

When they finally graduated, Lauren was already set to complete her studies at university and Shelley decided to take a year to decide what she would do. Most of her money was in trust until she was 21, but she didn't mind waiting.

When Lauren left for university, Robert encouraged Shelley to get an apartment with him and she happily agreed.

"I don't have money until I turn 21," she told him.

"That's okay sugar," he'd say, "I will take care of things."

Now, in their 20s, Lauren was about to graduate with honors and Shelley was still living with Robert. Robert had become a total loser. He'd go out for days at a time. He wouldn't even call. She'd also been taught NOT to question his decisions. His hand was mighty when she sassed him.

Lauren would email or text Shelley daily. They never missed a beat, yet Robert had become jealous of their friendship and would invade her privacy.

"Who are you talking to?" he'd asked.

"Lauren."

"What for, you already talked to her

yesterday."

"Robert...she's my best friend. We share everything!"

"Well, I am sick of her coming between us."

"She's not."

"You belong to me now, Shelley. I don't want you talking to her anymore."

"That's too bad, Robert," Shelley snapped. "I will talk to whom I chose."

"Not while I'm your man!"

"Then maybe you won't be my man anymore."

"You're not leaving me bitch!"

"Why should I stay?"

"Because I said so!"

"Well, I don't deserve to be treated like this. My parents would not have wanted this for me," she admitted.

"Too bad daddy's not here to save you!"

"Don't say that. You know how much I loved them and how much I miss them."

"Get over it."

"You don't get over something like that."

"Do it anyways."

"That's it Robert! I am leaving!"

"You may leave, but not the way you're thinking," he grunted.

With a solid backhand, he smacked her hard across the cheek, knocking her to the floor. Then, as she lay there dazed, he proceeded to kick her multiple times in the stomach, head, and chest. Then, he grabbed her by the throat and picked her up off the floor.

"Stand up bitch!" he shouted. "You think you're going to get away with leaving?"

"Stop it!" she screamed.

Then he pressed her against the wall with abrupt force. His hands gripped firmly on her neck. Then he pulled her forward and then slammed her against the wall again. She hit the back of her head and she could barely see straight. The room was still spinning when he grabbed her by the hair and began dragging her to the balcony.

"Don't do it Robert!" she begged. Then he moved her to the edge of the balcony where he began to shove her off. She kicked and fought with all her might. She screamed as neighbors gathered, watching helplessly.

"Someone...call the police!" someone shouted.

Then with all her might, she knew it was him, or her. He had her body half pressed over the balcony, but with all her inner strength, she kicked him so hard that he lost his footing and plunged helplessly down to the pavement below. The ten-story fall killed him immediately.

Shelley's body hovered helplessly for a moment until a neighbor broke down the door and helped her back up to where she was safe.

Her body was a mess. She was bleeding heavily from the head, nose, and ears. Her arm was swollen and bruised. She could barely speak before she passed out cold.

Two of the neighbors stayed with her, attending to her wounds. Not sure who to call, one of them picked up the phone and dialed the most frequently called number.

"Hi Shelley..." replied Lauren.

"I'm sorry, I'm not Shelley. I'm her neighbor Ethyl, from apartment 10 A," she said.

Lauren's heart sank. She'd often thought something was wrong between Robert and Shelley, but Shelley wouldn't talk about it. Still, when she heard Ethyl speak she became immediately concerned. "Has something happened?"

"Are you her family?" asked Ethyl.

"No, but she's been my best friend for almost 20 years."

"Oh dear, do you know how to reach her family?"

"I'm all she's got. Her family was killed 5 years ago in an accident. Can you please tell me what's happening?"

"Well, the ambulance is coming to get her and I'm afraid Robert's dead."

"What?"

Ethyl gave a quick recant of the story that had unfolded before them. Though most didn't see what led to the balcony horror, they did recognize that she was in danger and that Robert, in his attempt to kill her, had fallen and died.

Lauren didn't waste any time. She immediately got on the next plane and flew to be by Shelley's side. One look at her friend in the hospital bed and she shuddered. Shelley was still unconscious from the surgery, so Lauren sought the doctor for information on her health.

"Well, she did sustain a concussion and we had to remove her spleen. Her left wrist has a slight fracture," he explained.

She shuttered again. "And what about the law? Will there be charges pressed?"

"I don't know much about it, Miss Smith, but I do know that the witnesses are attesting it was self-defense," he explained. "I wouldn't worry too much about it. We have a lot of evidence to prove she'd been abused."

"Abused?" asked Lauren. "I suspected things weren't great, but didn't know to what extent."

"Well, she's been to the ER a few times for stitches, broken finger, and a cracked rib. According to what we read..." the doctor paused. "Simply put Miss Smith, she isn't likely to be charged."

"Glad to hear that. Can I sit with her

now?"

"Of course you can. She should be coming around soon."

Lauren sat down beside Shelley's bed and began to talk to her about "old times." She reminded her of their sunshine-filled days as kids, playing in the sand, tossing the ball around, and riding their bikes. Then, Lauren began to tell Shelley about how much she loved her. She didn't want to admit that it was a love-love feeling, but it was. She simply let Shelley know that their bond was endless and that she would do anything for her.

As Lauren continued to talk to Shelley, Shelley began to stir. Her eyes opened slowly and then she turned and smiled at Lauren's beautiful face.

"I love you too," she said.

"Oh Shelley!"

"I can't believe you're here," Shelley said.

"There's nowhere I'd rather be than with you."

"I feel the same way. Always have."

"We have a truly special friendship, don't we?"

"Definitely, but..." Shelley looked awkward. She'd looked that way once or twice in the past. Once at their high school prom. The other, on the day Lauren left for university.

"What's the matter?" Lauren asked.

"I've been lying to myself for a long, long time."

"About what?"

"About you, Lauren."

"Me?"

Shelley's eyes began to tear and her lip began to quiver.

"Shelley, what on earth is wrong?"

"Oh Lauren, when I said I loved you, I wasn't meaning like a sister or friend." Shelley gulped firmly, hoping that she hadn't made the biggest mistake of her life.

Lauren smiled. "You do?"

"Please, don't make me say it again," Shelley sobbed. "I am sorry if that bothered you. I didn't mean to..."

Immediately Lauren cut Shelley off and placed her fingers over her lips and said "Ssshh..." then lovingly, Lauren leaned over and gently kissed Shelley's swollen lips. "I love you too..."

Shelley stared in awe.

"I've love-loved you since I was about sixteen. It's why I never dated. I wanted to take you to the prom so badly, but..."

"I can't believe this!" Shelley sniffed. "I've felt that way a long time too..."

"Oh Shelley, I'm so glad this is out now. Now there's only one thing to do."

"What's that?"

"Get you better, so I can take you home with me!"

"I'd like that!" she said.

After a week in the hospital, Lauren was finally able to take Shelley home. And to her undying pleasure and devotion, Lauren catered to Shelley attentively until she fully recovered.

Shelley welcomed the hugs and kisses, and really enjoyed the cuddles, but her body had not been ready for much more than that until now.

Feeling as well as she had felt previously, Shelley decided to create a romantic experience for her and her partner. Her 21st birthday was only a week away and the one thing she knew for sure is that she loved Lauren and wanted her for life.

Carefully, Shelley prepared a delicious meal consisting of all of Lauren's favorite food. She made a roasted chicken dinner, with snow peas and roasted potatoes. Dessert was a delicious chocolate torte. Then, she carefully sprinkled rose petals along the floor of her bedroom and across the queen-sized bed. With a bottle of chilled champagne sitting nearby, candles, and serene music, the stage was set.

As Lauren opened the door, she was immediately caught away by the fragrance of delicious food and vanilla-scented candles. Then, seeing the eloquently decorated table for two, she smiled.

Shelley met her in the room and smiled. "Welcome home, Lauren," she said.

"This is exquisite Shelley!"

"This is all for you."

Lauren was moved to tears. A slight trickle of passion dropped upon her cheek, but Shelley knew by the immense smile that it was a tear of joy.

"Come," Shelley gestured. "I've prepared all your favorites."

Lauren was swept away. Every morsel was deeply satisfying, but the sweet, tender-caring attention was even tastier.

"I can't believe you went to so much trouble."

"Wait, there's more..."

Lauren couldn't imagine what the "more" was going to be, but she was eager to find out. "Come..." Shelley said again.

Shelley delicately took Lauren by the hand and led her to the bedroom. The notion was clear. Words didn't need to be spoken here. Passionately, Lauren took Shelley by the hand and laid her across the mattress.

"Are you ready to do this?" Lauren asked.

Shelley said nothing, but instead sealed her answer with a kiss. Suddenly the passion of their love took over. Their kiss grew with intensity and heat, their tongues sliding inside one another's mouths. Shelley was wearing nothing more than a silk teddy and robe. Lauren began to move her hands down the smooth fabric and gently caressed Shelley's breast. She continued to kiss Shelley and massage her perky nipple, while Shelley maneuvered her hands to unbutton Lauren's blouse.

As she found her way into the blouse, she slid her hand across her Lauren's breast and returned the gesture. Then, carefully, she used her hands to assist in removing the blouse. Shelley continued to undo the skirt Lauren was wearing and moved her fingers into her panties, teasing the pussy slightly.

Then Lauren slipped her hands under the silk teddy and lifted it over Shelley's head, leaving nothing but the panties.

As Shelley continued to aid Lauren in removing the skirt, she massaged gently along her silky thighs and buttocks.

Lauren began to lick Shelley's neck and then moved down towards the stomach. Then, as she gently slipped her fingers around the panties, she gently slipped them down and off. Without reservation, she began to gently caress the clit with her tongue. Shelley laid back and surrendered to the loving touch.

Lauren's touch was sensual and erotic. Shelley's body tensed with euphoria as her back arched with delight. The relentless cries of heat and passion exuded her mouth as each stroke of the tongue moved the climax to complete height. Shelley's eyes rolled back in her head as she let out a pitiful cry of orgasmic release. Her heart was pounding, but without hesitation, she laid Lauren back upon the bed and began to lick along the insides of the thigh, teasing the pussy slightly with breezy little passes.

Then finally, she removed Lauren's panties and began to lick the clitoris seductively. Her fingers slipped gently into her vagina and massaged the wall, while her tongue continued to delight Lauren's eager clitoris.

With each lick of the "magic spot," Lauren's body tingled and groaned with sensual anticipation. She grabbed her breasts and held them in place while her eyes rolled around, seeking the moment of final release. Then with one final sweet touch from Shelley's tongue, Lauren released a joyful cry.

Returning to the surface, Shelley looked Lauren in the eye and their love had reached a new height, a height they hadn't thought possible. As Shelley crawled upon the bed beside Lauren, she caressed her naked body softly while gazing in her eyes.

"Lauren?" she said.

"Yeah?"

"I can't imagine one day of my life, without you in it."

"I agree," said Lauren.

"Then do me the honor of becoming my partner in life?"

"Are you asking me what I think you're asking me?"

"Yes Lauren. I am asking if you'll marry me."

Lauren smiled. "I can't imagine a better way to finish this day. You, Shelley, are the love of my life. From the time we played sandcastles together with our tiny red shovels, to now. There's nothing I'd love more to do than spend my life with you..."

"Is that a yes then?"

"Yes, dear Shelley, that is a definite yes!"

Joy had filled their hearts from an unexpected turn of events. From their days of playing with shovels in the sand to this day of making passionate love, their lives had come full circle, and it was good. Damn good!

9 FASHION TOIS

Felicity Dulcet was a high-end fashion designer for Keriway Fashions. Known and admired by her peers, Felicity was making her mark on every runway in the world. Her studio was often full of gorgeous models - both male and female - all anxious to wear her designer labels. From lingerie to full-scale runway gowns, her taste for the extraordinary was, without a doubt, sensational.

Two of her best models were Kristopher Conway and Derek Forman, both of whom wore her clothing not only as models but in the "real world" too. The clothing was always made from the highest-quality French or Italian fabrics. No garment was ever "cheaply" made. In fact, three of

Felicity's gowns were worn at the most recent Academy awards. It was known, without a doubt, that Felicity had arrived. Her gowns on the red carpet? She couldn't have imagined a better feeling.

At the age of six, Felicity was discovered in her rat-infested apartment by the landlord, abandoned. Nobody ever knew how long she'd been there, but she'd had a leash tied to her ankle and secured to a table leg, with only a few boxes of dry cereal. The child had tried to relieve herself at one end of the room while maintaining a somewhat orderly space on the other side of the room. She had fashioned herself a small bed with a throw cushion and towel.

Had it not been for the smell of rotting food on the dining room table, nobody would have found her in time to save her from certain death.

When asked why she hadn't called for help, she told them she was supposed to stay quiet or she would "get it." She spent three days in the hospital and was treated for dehydration, infected bug bites, urine sores, and malnourishment. It took even longer still to heal the mental effects of the cruelty she'd been subjected to.

Child Protective Services couldn't find a home for her; nobody wanted "that kind of trouble." Then, at fifteen, her best friend Emily's family invited her to stay with them for a while. There she received some much needed values, love, and nurturing. She successfully completed high school and gained a scholarship to Parson's in New York City. Then she studied abroad in Paris and Italy, two years consecutively.

Yet, while she studied abroad, she received news that Emily had been killed in a car wreck and her life was shattered again. Despite all her trials and woes, Felicity persevered, focusing on her success. And now, the fruits of her labor glimmered endlessly on magazine covers and Hollywood runways—a bittersweet victory.

"Okay guys, we need to get you all into your outfits. What's taking so long!" she barked as the hustle and bustle of the pre-runway show chaotically took on a life of its own. Jillian was undoubtedly one of her best-looking models, but also one of the biggest pains in the ass she had. Always late, always sassy, and always willing to bitch at anyone who got in her way.

"Where's Jillian?" Felicity shouted.

"Don't know?" replied her assistant.

"It's your job to know this, Cam!"

"I've checked her room twice, texted her seven times, and still..."

"Call her!"

"I'm here, Felicity." Jillian chimed as she walked into the studio.

"Damn it Jillian! You have to be ready to go on in eight minutes!"

"Take a chill pill, Felicity," Jillian replied. "I'm here now."

"Ah!" Felicity wanted so many times to fire the bitch, but the crowd and cameras loved her. The problem was—Jillian knew it!

As she prepped the finishing touches of her models, she took a final look at Kris and Derek. "Aw boys, you always do me proud!" she said. "Hmm hmm!"

"Happy to serve you, Felicity," Kris said.

"Great, now get those yummy asses up there on that runway and show them what we've got!"

"You got it, Felicity!" Derek said in his soft retort.

And they were off!

One after another after another, the garments lit up the runway, hungered by the call of the perfect rhythm. She always loved the flashing lights, both the camera lights and the colorful strobe lights. It energized her. The audience ate it up and the investors were thrilled.

"Another amazing show, Felicity!" Jade said.

"Aw thanks," she said. "Couldn't have done it without this amazing team!"

The fashions were amazing and the magazines were there for the scoop of the day.

With the show over, Jillian left on her high horse while the others simply returned to a more "normal" façade. While it was always good practice looking good every now and then, it was nice just to be casual.

"Great show guys!" she told them all.

"Love this outfit," Derek said. "Makes my ass look perdy."

"Luscious, Derek. Yum!" Kris said.

Derek and Kristopher were openly gay, happy to be gay and didn't care who knew. While both men were incredibly hot, all the girls knew they were out of bounds.

Kristopher was 5'11" and thin, but built. He had gorgeous brown curls and scruff on his face. Derek, on the other hand was 6'3" tall, had a short, almost bald haircut and a thin beard. They were rarely apart. They lived together, worked together, and raised their loving cat Ralphy—named after Ralph Lauren.

Kristopher didn't appear as "obviously gay" as Derek. Yet the slight indicators did lean towards his sexual lifestyle. Derek, however, was about as gay as they come. He...how do they say it... "talked the talk and walked the walk." Both men were comfortably gay. If you didn't like them, it was "talk to the hand" and move on.

After a wonderful evening of post-show celebrating, everyone had seemingly gone home. Gus the security guard was making his rounds, while Felicity finished putting away some of the garments.

"Damn that Cam! She never does this right. Guess it's time for another assistant."

While she continued to put the items away, she could hear some commotion coming from the auditorium. She casually slipped into the arena and was immediately shocked to find Kristopher and Derek fucking one another on the runway.

"Oh shit!" she gasped.

They both stopped and stared in horror.

"I'm sorry," she cried, as she covered her eyes.

"Don't be sorry," Kristopher said. "Nothing to be ashamed of here. Just love."

"But on the runway?" she asked.

"Oh dearie, you haven't lived until you've fucked on a runway after a show," Derek explained.

Felicity was intrigued. "Really?"

"Want to find out?" Derek asked.

"Shush, Derek! That's our boss!"

Felicity looked around to make sure they were alone. "What the hell, you only live once, right?"

The men smiled and welcomed her openly.

Boldly, Felicity approached the runway and immediately surrendered her body to their will. Kristopher, the one who was more willing to cross the gender line, began to run his fingers up her thigh and up under her skirt. He had a very pleasing touch, and she immediately began to feel the sensational play.

Then, discovering her tiny thong, he moved his fingers along the string and slipped them down into the Brazilian-waxed pussy. The skin was soft and supple, the slow teasing increasing her arousal. While Kristopher continued to please her pussy, Derek stood up and began moving his hands up under her blouse. He unbuttoned the $400 garment. Carefully, he slipped it off her shoulders and then gingerly moved his fingers to the back of her bra, where he deliberately unhooked the clasp.

Immediately her voluptuous breasts were exposed, and he lovingly and delicately began to massage them with his hands, one breast in each. Then without hesitation, they moved closer. He began to suck on her ear lobe and then moved his mouth over to hers. Their lips locked and his tongue slipped into her mouth. Graciously, she accepted the penetration and returned the favor with her own tongue.

But her breathing began to become more labored as Kristopher removed her panties, slipping them off over her stilettos. Then, moving her skirt upward, he moved his tongue to her pussy and delicately separated the lips, exposing the clitoris within.

Felicity's body began to tense with erotic pleasure. His tongue then slipped along the clit and began massaging it teasingly while his fingers slipped into the vagina and moved boldly upwards. Her whole body was being caressed and it felt fucking good.

She could barely stand, so, carefully, the two men laid her body upon the ground and then they continued to pleasure the beautiful woman. Derek placed his mouth upon the left breast and tenderly licked the nipple, sucking and nipping it gently, keeping it erected.

Kristopher then moved his hands along her thighs and carefully moved her legs apart, then returned his tongue to her clitoris and proceeded to stroke it. Her sense of pleasure began to move her body into a state of climatic euphoria. Her back arched as her hands gripped for the flesh of Derek's back. Her eyes rolled erratically back and forth until they climatically moved deep into the back of her head. Her cries and moans nearly shook the rafters above them.

She cried and panted, moaned and screamed as Kristopher's tongue finally hit the magic peak, releasing the orgasm within. Her heart pounded hard as her pussy tingled with the erotic aftermath of the orgasm.

"Fucking amazing!" she cried. "Fucking amazing!"

Then realizing her two mates were in need of some fucking, she rose to her knees. She unzipped Derek's pants and helped move them to the floor, along with the briefs beneath them. Then Kristopher stood firmly in place behind Derek and carefully prepared the rectum for penetration.

With Derek's hardened cock exposed, Felicity slipped her mouth around the point and teased the tip delicately, extenuating the ecstasy. Then, while she continued to encourage Derek's pleasure, Kristopher moved his cock delicately forward and slid it into Derek's rectum.

While Felicity sucked the cock with some vigor and some tease, Kristopher continued to slip his cock back and forth within the anal cavity, with repeated strokes—each stroke gaining more momentum and depth. The arousing pleasure from both sides of his body made Derek's whole body tingle with excitement. Kristopher could feel the tension around his own cock and moaned delightfully as he moved. His hands slipped to the front of Derek's body and gripped his chest for balance.

Felicity continued to suck the cock harder and harder, moving her tongue around it, providing the moist pleasure. Derek's feet gripped the runway as his hands held fast to his partner's hands, trying to remain firmly planted on the floor.

But for the amazing sensation of ecstasy in both the cock and rectal region, Derek pounded harder and harder. His breathing increased with every amazing motion. Then with two more savory sucks, Derek's cum rushed from the cannon and oozed swiftly into Felicity's mouth.

Kristopher's moment was about to peak, as he firmly held Derek in place. Kris moved back and forth, faster and faster, deeper and deeper; then finally, with an earth-shattering moan of ecstasy, Kristopher's cock ejaculated the thick salty substance and then carefully extracted from Derek's rectum.

The three of them lay naked upon the runway, draped only in a tablecloth, their bodies embracing the rush of their three-way orgy. Felicity lay delicately against Kristopher's chest, while Derek laid his head upon her lap.

"I must say, Derek, you were right," she said.

"About what?"

"This. This was fucking amazing!"

"It was, wasn't it?"

“I don’t know if it was just being with you two or if it was the knowledge that we were fucking on the runway—out where Gus could have found us.”

“I think it’s likely both. There is something to be said for risk, but there’s also something to be said for knowing how to please someone,” Kristopher said.

“Oh, and baby… you sure do!”

“You do a pretty good job of that yourself, Felicity,” Derek said.

“Well, I don’t know about you two,” she said. “But I think you may have started something here.”

“Maybe we have,” said Derek, “are you thinking of having seconds?”

“Seconds?” she asked. “I’m thinking of having a fucking buffet!”

“Now that does sound like a plan!”

While Felicity wasn’t into the whole “relationship” part of their special arrangement, she was certainly into the influx of pleasure. From then on, as a standing arrangement, any night a show had occurred, they would meet for their runway rendezvous and enjoy a moment of fashion lovemaking.

“Life is pretty amazing now,” or so she thought. Her fashions were taking off and making their mark, and she’d found a relationship that worked perfectly for her. No commitment was necessary, just sex, and that was fucking perfect!

10 FROM TEARS TO CHEERS

Jesse and Ryan Boss have been married for just a little over three years. They lived in a three-story mansion in Beverly Hills. Ryan, a feisty young executive, works tirelessly for the always popular 'Kinkaid' hotel chains and resorts. His wife, Jesse worked for Paul Kaminski, one of Hollywood's most respected and sought-after criminal attorneys.

Paul's wife, Alicia worked as a chef at the "Silver Pearl," a five star dining establishment. People book months in advance just to get in. Her passion for food shone through each and every time she plated the succulent morsels, and her pastries were to die for!

Now, Alicia had once been engaged to

Ryan, and while they did eventually break up, their passion for one another was never fully extinguished. Despite the awkward history, Jesse was able to work untarnished for Paul and enjoyed doing so.

One day, Jesse had gotten home early and discovered Ms. Gertrude Firestone, her neighbor standing in her driveway.

"Oh shit, what does that nosey broad want now?" she wondered.

As she shut off the car, Ms. Gertrude Firestone eagerly ran over, dying to share whatever gossip she had scooped up that day. As she ran towards her, her enormous hooters bounced about freely. "Damn, doesn't she own a bra?!" Jesse wondered.

The woman had to be easily 400 lbs., always wore loud garments—that looked more like disgusting table cloths—and her hair was usually up in rollers.

"Jesse! Jesse!" she shouted as she waved her hands and flabby arms about.

"Hello Ms. Firestone," Jesse said as she opened the car door and stepped out, "What's new?"

"Oh Jesse, Jesse, Jesse," she babbled. "I'm so sorry to be the one to break the news to you dear."

Jesse rolled her eyes, discretely. "What news?"

"Well dear, I saw your husband today..."

she began.

"Okay?"

"He was with...her."

"Her who?" Jesse's eyebrow raised a little, curiously.

"You know, that Alicia woman," she said.

"Umm, okay?" Jesse didn't much like their "friendship," but she didn't want to be known as the jealous type, so if she overheard someone say they'd seen them at Starbuck's, she would simply shrug it off. But not this time.

"Well dear, I saw them at Bark's Jewelry store," she said.

"She was helping him put on a men's bracelet," explained Ms. Firestone.

"Oh, okay," Jesse said. "Thanks for letting me know."

"Dear, don't you see?" she asked. "He's having a fling. Oh, why is it always the wife's the last to know these things? I'm just sorry I had to be the one to tell you. I hate have to do that sort of thing."

"Sure you do, Ms. Firestone."

"What's that mean?"

"Oh nothing."

"Well, dear, if you need a shoulder to cry on, I'll be right here, okay?"

"I'm sure it's nothing Ms. Firestone. I trust Ryan."

"Of course you do dear. Of course you do." Ms. Firestone seemed quite sarcastically sympathetic. Then with a pat on the shoulder, Ms. Firestone walked back to her house. Jesse just shook her head.

"What a busy body!" she groaned as she entered the house, shutting the door behind her.

While Jesse knew that Ms. Firestone's "gossip scoops" were pretty much nothing more than bullshit, she couldn't quite get this tidbit out of her mind. "Why was Ryan with Alicia? What was the bracelet for?" She really didn't know, but she was certain Ryan was innocent of anything inappropriate. "Besides, he'll tell me about his rendezvous with Alicia when he gets home. I'm sure he will!"

Convinced it was all just a strange, drummed up pile of bullshit, Jesse continued on with her evening duties and began to sort through her bills, while supper was being made.

First, she paid the phone bill, and then she opened the Visa bill. "$500 for earrings?" she gasped. She thought for a moment that maybe he'd bought them for her for a special occasion, but there wasn't one coming up. Her birthday was four months earlier, Christmas was still a few months away, and their anniversary had just past too. She tried not to dwell on it, but her mind kept returning to Ms. Firestone's little tidbit.

Tortured and annoyed, she continually tried to shake off the negative emotions, but simply couldn't escape it.

Finally, after a few hours of pacing the floor, Jesse could hear Ryan's car pulling into the driveway. She peeped out her window, looking to see who was around. "Geesh," she said to herself, "I've turned into Ms. Firestone, snooping like this."

She felt silly.

Ryan hadn't noticed her peeping and soon entered the home "normally." Then seeing the look on Jesse's face, he got worried. "Something wrong?" he asked.

"No…" she hesitated. "Nothing's wrong, why?"

"I don't know," he said. "You just look…hmm…can't put my finger on it."

"Oh, it's nothing, really. Just thinking."

"Uh oh," he hummed. "This doesn't involve moving any furniture, does it?"

"No. Nothing like that dear." Then, changing the topic she asked, "You hungry?"

"Yep, I am. What's that smell?"

"Chili."

"Okay, sounds good."

"Not quite as good as Alicia's cooking though, is it?"

Suddenly, Ryan's face went white. "Why would you bring her up?"

"Oh, no reason…"

"You're cooking's fine Jess," he said. "I

know it's not five star, but I'm not a five-star guy."

"So, what did you do today?" she asked.

"Worked, of course," he replied. Then, judging by the look on her face, he wondered if he'd forgotten a special occasion. "Nope, not our anniversary, birthday, nope...hmm..." he could not figure out why she had such an attitude with him.

"Did you have anything exciting happen?"

"No, just sat in my office and worked the whole day."

Now, Jesse was really mad. She caught him in a lie, but wasn't about to let him get away with it that easily. "Well, enjoy your dinner." she huffed as she plopped the plate of chili upon the table.

"What' with you tonight Jesse?"

"Nothing. Goodnight! I'm tired!"

With a hmm, a hah, and a huff, Jesse stormed back up to her room and simply went to bed. She wanted to cry, but was too damn mad to. "I'll get even with him!"

She left Ryan's blanket and pillow in the hallway outside the bedroom door; apparently, he was sleeping on the couch, but he really didn't know why. As he tossed and turned, she plotted and schemed. "Cheat on me you bastard!" she groaned. "I'll show you!"

Paul was working on a case when Jesse showed up at the office. Amber, his secretary, buzzed his office.

"Yes Amber?" he asked.

"Sir, I have a Jesse Boss here, wanting to meet with you," she said.

"Oh sure, you can send her in."

Hanging up the phone, Amber said, "Right this way."

As she opened the door to the office, Jesse became nervous. She wondered if she was making a fool of herself, yet she could not escape the frustration she was dealing with inside.

"Hello Jesse, what can I do for you?" Paul asked as she stepped into his office.

Jesse looked around and then closed the door. Then, locked it behind her. Paul looked confused.

"Is anything the matter Jesse?"

"Oh, no," she said. "Nothing really at all..." Then looking seductively at him, she moved slowly towards him, letting down her long dark hair. Her big brown eyes sparkling with lust and purpose. Her powerful stride made him nervous.

"Jesse?" he gulped. "What are you doing?"

"Isn't it obvious Paul?"

"Kind of," he gulped again.

"Come on Paul, you know you think I'm hot..."

"Well, yes you are, but..." Her long silky

legs, killer smile, her supple lips, and curvy hips, all made for a tempting treat. "But what about..."

"Shh, Paul, don't ruin the moment."

Her seductive charm and enticing good looks became irresistible. He could barely control himself. Then she teasingly slipped her hand upon his crotch and held his package firmly, yet gently. She smiled. Her seduction was definitely causing an arousal.

"Well, well, well..." she said. "I think someone's happy I came."

He gulped again. His head said no, but his balls said "Oh Yeah!"

Eagerly, she began to unzip his pants and then delicately moved her body down towards his thickly erected cock. His heart pounded, with fear he'd get caught and with pleasure for how good she was making him feel.

She carefully began to stroke his dick and blew teasingly upon it, and then standing up again, she began to take off her blouse and then her brazier, revealing her youthful, full-sized breasts. The pink nipples were perked and tastefully beautiful. Then, encouraging his effort, she took his hands and placed them upon her breasts.

"You like?"

He gulped again, nervously.

"Well, do you?"

He nodded timidly.

She smiled as he slowly began to stroke the nipples with his thumbs. She moaned slightly, enforcing her purpose for being there.

Then, he moved his left hand down her side and placed it upon her perfectly formed buttocks, grabbing it firmly and pulling her closer to him. Then, as he became increasingly aroused, he slipped his hand up under her skirt and went in search of her very fine pussy.

She raised her leg and wrapped it around his body, allowing him easier access to her genital area. Then carefully, he began to move his fingers around her clit, causing her heart to begin pounding and releasing the sweet crying moans. He continued to move his fingers to her vaginal area and slipped around to gather some of the surfacing fluid. Excited to see her eyes rolling around, he began to move his fingers more teasingly around her clitoris.

Then as she became fully aroused, she slipped down, teasingly sucked his dick, and then aided him in dropping his pants.

Without any further hesitation, Paul lifted the gorgeous woman, laid her upon his office sofa, and then proceeded to insert his cock. She arched with delight as he penetrated the opening. Now, fully intact, Paul began to throttle his cock back and forth, increasing the pleasure for both of them. Knowing that Amber was just in the next room, they kept their panting and moan to a minimum. Yet, as the hearty thrusts continued to elevate the ecstasy of pleasure, the climactic moment surged to the ceiling, releasing them both of the joy of orgasm.

Finally, they were done, but neither said a word. It was quiet for a moment while they both tidied themselves up, but words were simply best left, unspoken.

Later that night, Alicia and Paul were dining at home, when she presented him with a gift. He smiled, but wondered what the occasion was. Then, as he opened the tiny box, his mind returned to the moment of indiscretion he'd had with Jesse, hoping Alicia would never know.

Inside the elegant box was a gold link bracelet, engraved with his initials and on the back it said "Love Always, Alicia." Now, he really felt bad. The bracelet was beautiful, but he'd fucked up, big time!"

"This is beautiful," he said with a smile.

"Oh thank you. I had Ryan help me pick it out," she confessed.

"Oh, I see," Paul was feeling really awkward, but worked hard at hiding it. He was a lawyer after all, sidestepping the truth was part of his job; surely, she would not know what he'd done.

Meanwhile, back in Ryan and Jesse's

home, Jesse was feeling pretty good about her act of revenge. As Ryan walked into the house, he looked at his wife and wondered why she looked so coy, yet, not wanting to jinx things, he simply ignored it.

"Hi Jesse," he said. "Did you have a good day?"

"Pretty good, yeah. How about you?"

"Well, it was good."

"Anything exciting happen?" she asked.

"Other than picking up a bracelet for Alicia," He paused, "Not really."

"What bracelet?"

"The other day, I helped her pick out a bracelet for Paul. It was to celebrate his new partnership at the firm."

"The bracelet was for Paul?" Jesse felt terrible. "What have I done?" Her heart sunk like a rock. The guilt was almost overwhelming, so to alleviate the burden, she immediately scurried around the house, making sure Ryan felt loved.

Jesse felt like shit. She really fucked things up. She only hoped it wouldn't come back to bite her in the ass.

The next morning, Alicia went to Paul's work to surprise him with some yummy morsels from her restaurant. Amber was not at her desk, so she carefully knocked on the door to his office. There was no answer. Curiously, she opened the door and walked in.

She figured she could wait a little while.

As she sat down upon the sofa, her hand came across something she had not been prepared to find. As she grabbed the object and held it up, she gawked in dismay. “A bra!”

Alarmed and dismayed, she began to wonder who had been in her husband’s office. Who had lost her brazier? “Maybe it belongs to Amber?”

Seeing her back at her desk, Alicia exited the office and approach Amber immediately. Amber smiled, unprepared for what Alicia would say. “Is this yours Amber?” She held up the bra and the look on Amber’s face said she knew something.

“No ma’am it’s not mine. It’s far too big for me!”

“But you know who it belongs to, don’t you?”

“I...umm...” Amber was a terrible liar.

“Out with it!”

“Mrs. Kaminski, I am not permitted to disclose matters that happen behind Mr. Kaminski’s door,” she replied.

“This isn’t a matter of law; this is a matter of my marriage!”

“I can’t tell you who they belonged to, but if you look carefully at the garment, I think you might have an idea already....”

Alicia did just that. She looked carefully and realized that there was someone this brazier would fit. “Jesse?” she wondered, as she eyed Amber carefully.

Amber gulped awkwardly.

"Okay Amber, you didn't say anything...at least not with your mouth."

Immediately, Alicia stormed out of the office and drove straight to Jesse's home. Her mind was racing with how she was going to handle it. As soon as Jesse opened the door, she saw the brazier dangling from Alicia's hand. Jesse froze.

"Oh Alicia!" she cried. "I can explain!"

"Really? I've got to hear this!"

Jesse immediately went through the suspicions she'd had with Alicia and Ryan, and how Ms. Firestone had planted the seed of stupidity. As Jesse fumbled over her words, Alicia almost "understood."

"I'd do anything to make this right!" she said.

While Alicia and Jesse were "talking things over," Paul arrived back at his office. When he entered the room, he had found the container full of gourmet food. He stepped back out and asked, "Amber?"

"Yes sir?"

"Was my wife here?"

"Yes sir," she gulped. "And she knows sir..."

"Knows what?"

"About you know...her..." Amber was terrible at "beating around the bush."

"She knows!?"

"She found the brazier..."

"Oh shit!"

He immediately left the office and ran for his car, as he was about to get into the car he ran into Ryan.

"Hey, ready to play some racket ball?"

"Damn it Ryan," he gasped. "Get in the car! I need to stop my wife from killing your wife!"

"What the hell are you talking about?"

"I'll explain on the way," Paul said.

They drove straightway to Ryan and Jesse's house, hoping to defuse a brutal situation. Ryan was furious with Paul and Jesse. He'd been betrayed, yet, for the moment, he agreed to stop the feud he expected to find.

When they arrived at the house, it seemed quiet. Nervously, Ryan fumbled for the keys and then the two men walked inside. Alicia's shoes and purse were at the door, but there was no sign of either woman.

Then all of a sudden, they heard a pitiful cry.

"Quick! Upstairs!" Ryan shouted.

The two men charged up the stairs and burst effortlessly into Jesse and Ryan's room. Suddenly, both men stopped cold. They could scarcely believe their eyes.

There, in the matrimonial bed, was Alicia and Jesse. They were both completely naked, and their clothing was scattered around the room. Neither man knew what to say. They looked at one another with jaws gawking wide.

Ryan was stunned. "What the fuck is going on here?"

"Honey!" Jesse shouted.

"Don't honey me," he snapped.

"Listen Ryan," Alicia said. "There's room in here for two more, ya know?" She winked teasingly as she patted the bed.

Paul looked at Ryan and then back at the two stunning women. "You know, maybe in this case, it is better to join them, huh?" Paul quickly ripped off his clothing and bounded towards his wife. "You coming too, aren't you?"

Ryan stood there for at least thirty seconds and said nothing. Then realizing his options and the joys of this challenge, he willingly threw off his garments and dodged for the middle of the bed. Between the licking and sucking, moaning and groaning, the pleasures went on for hours. Though their household secret would remain a mystery to the world, their newfound "appreciation" shifted the tears of sorrow and made way for a new kind of reconciliation.

Then later that evening, as they all sat down to enjoy some of Alicia's fanciful cooking, they lifted their glasses in unanimous collaboration and toasted one another. "Cheers," they said in unison as their glasses clanged. Sometimes when playing poker, the best hand you can play is two pair.

AUTHOR'S NOTE

Readers: I want to expand a few of the stories to see where the characters can be explored further. If there are any of the stories that you would like to read more about again, I'd love to hear from you!

Visit my blog at
http://www.emiliehamdan.com

Join my newsletter for free exclusive previews
http://www.emiliehamdan.com/in

Follow me on Twitter at
http://www.twitter.com/emiliehamdan

Like my page on Facebook at
http://www.facebook.com/emiliehamdan

Discover my books at major ebook retailers everywhere.

www.ingramcontent.com/pod-product-compliance
Lightning Source LLC
LaVergne TN
LVHW041929090826
845145LV00017B/2318

* 9 7 8 1 6 2 3 2 7 5 5 0 1 *